PERSONAL DISASTER

AINSLEY BOOTH

SHE'S LOOKING FOR A STORY ABOUT A BILLIONAIRE. HE'S THE PARK RANGER STANDING IN HER WAY.

Ten years ago, Marcus Dane left the tech world in his dust and joined the National Park Service. For the last decade, the world has ignored the park ranger-who-could-have-been-a-billionaire, but now an intrepid reporter has tracked him down. Worse, Poppy Lisowski has a theory about him which could blow his quiet life to smithereens. He needs to send her packing. But he's already tumbled head-over-heels in insta-lust with her flippy ponytail and smart mouth...

For Emma

CHAPTER ONE

MARCUS

July
Rifle, Colorado

I HAVE GREAT FRIENDS. But they're also jerks, and I tell them as much when they call me as a group from the Hamptons.

It turns out two of them have big news.

"Had you told me that you were getting engaged, I'd have maybe flown out for the weekend," I tell Jake Aston. And you..." I point at Toby Hunt, who's sporting a giant shit-eating grin. "Married?"

Ben Russo shakes his head on my phone's screen. "I know. They both kept good secrets. Too good. Sorry you aren't here, man."

"Yeah, well..." I flip the camera around on my own phone

and show them the mountain top I'm currently looking at across a gorge just outside my office. "That's my view, you assholes, so I'm not too sad."

They howl with laughter, then Jake makes me promise to come back out east for the wedding.

"I wouldn't miss it for the world. Now I have to get back to work. Leave me alone," I growl. But I'm grinning, and that smile doesn't drop off my face until I arrive back at the National Park Service-owned cabin where I work.

Whoever she is, the stacked brunette with the perky ponytail and open-toed sandals peering in the windows of my office isn't from around here. Which is a shame, because I like perky ponytails.

The sandals are an interesting choice in the Rocky Mountains, but to each their own.

I don't like industrious outsiders who drive halfway up a mountain to find me, though.

And I don't need to make it easy for her now.

"Can I help you?" I ask in that *probably not, but say your piece anyway* voice that usually sends people running.

She straightens and turns around, a polite smile on her face. "Perhaps you can. I'm looking for Marcus Dane. Do you know him?"

Like I'm your stereotypical bearded mountain man who knows everyone in the national park, but couldn't possible be the guy she's looking for. She's right on the former point, and too bad for her, very wrong on the latter.

"Not sure anyone really knows Marcus Dane."

"That's what I've heard."

Well that's not good. "Are you here on official business or..."

I leer at her, because it's both effective and fun. When was the last time I got a good leer in? College, probably. "Something more personal?"

Sadly, the leer I'm so proud of doesn't send her shrieking for the hills. She gives me a bland look and hands over a business card. "Business, Mr. Dane. Nice beard, by the way. Killer disguise."

I sigh as I read the card. Her name is Poppy Lisowski and she's a journalist. Her card lists a few different places she's been published. I recognize The Washington Record, and I think Poindexter is a blog I've heard about on the morning news.

So she's not here about anything good, then.

"It's not a disguise," I say slowly, taking my time so I can figure out something, anything more about her. "It's just my face. Which you looked at and appeared not to recognize, and since I was just about to take a coffee break, Ms. Lisowski, I thought I'd better find out if your reason for being here was more important than caffeine."

"Do you use Twitter, Mr. Dane?"

Ah. That kind of question. I take a deep breath and cross my arms over my chest. "That's none of your God damned business."

CHAPTER TWO

POPPY

THE BEARD definitely helps him look pissed off. It's close-cropped, so I can see the hard cut of his jaw as he grits his teeth. He's clearly uncomfortable with being hunted down, and part of me feels bad—just for a second—about poking this particular bear.

It's not like I don't have sympathy for the ideals he claims to protect. It's just that the truth is more important than political ideology.

I take a deep breath and try again. "Do you know Toby Hunt?"

"We went to college together."

"And you have visited him in San Francisco recently." Not a question. I've done my research.

"Technically he lives in Palo Alto, not San Francisco."

"Thank you for confirming your close relationship—"

"Go away, Ms. Lisowski. Nothing good will come of your nosing around here." He drops his hands to his sides, and the muscles in his shoulders bunch and roll, big and strong.

How big and strong he is doesn't matter in the least. I shouldn't notice that he's super tall, either. I'm not short, and he dwarfs me. So it's not the smartest idea to march forward and get right into his space, but that's what I do. I pull out my recorder, and ignoring the obvious shake in my hand, I turn it on. "Would you repeat that on the record?"

He leans in, his brown eyes sparkling for a split second before he shutters his gaze and directs his voice to the mic. "Go. Away. Ms. Lisowski."

"And the threat?"

"I didn't threaten you."

"You said nothing good will come of me nosing around here."

"Mighty big stretch to call that a threat." He shrugs. "But sure, I said that. On the record and everything."

"What do you mean, nothing good?"

He straightens up and props his hands on his hips now. He's constantly in motion, this park ranger. This rebel. This likely resistance leader. "What do you think you're going to find here, little one?"

I roll my eyes. First he tried to perv on me—which totally didn't work—and now he's being condescending? "You need to work on your scare tactics."

He grins unexpectedly. "But you are little."

"Not to most people."

"Ah." He winks. "Well, Poppy. I think you're going to

discover I am not most people. Now, I've decided this conversation isn't more important than caffeine, so if you'll excuse me, it's my coffee break."

He brushes past me and heads into his office.

That's his prerogative, but I wouldn't be a half-decent reporter if I left it at that. Also, there's no way I'd be able to justify my flight to Colorado.

I've got two options. I can chase after him and keep asking him questions he doesn't want to answer, or I can wait him out.

I like door number two.

I plop my butt down on the porch outside his little log building and pull out my phone. I wonder what Mr. Alt Park Service is tweeting about right now?

They're all the same, these alt accounts. Morally outraged, full of righteous indignation. Half of them shams to drum up extremist rhetoric and disguise the rapid dismantling of the bureaucratic state. The other half are preaching to the choir. That story has been written. It's inspiring for the liberal base, and intriguing for journalists—for a hot minute.

But now *what* he's tweeting isn't nearly as important as *where* he's tweeting from—this particular account gave a couple of subtle and accidental clues in early tweets, right after the election, that point to this group of national parks west of Denver—and *how* he's doing it without getting caught.

Also, given the connections I've discovered in his background, *who* has helped him along the way.

Marcus Dane has some very wealthy friends.

Are the rules different when you're besties with billionaires?

While I wait for him to tweet, or not tweet, because maybe I've pissed him off and he's going to try and throw me off his scent, I pull up the dossier I've compiled on him.

I can't concentrate on the words, though. There's no *maybe* about the pissing him off part. I've definitely gotten under his skin. I pushed a little too hard.

Besides, I don't need to go over the dossier again. I've memorized every single word in it.

Marcus Dane went to MIT, where he met and befriended Jake Aston and Toby Hunt, when they were ordinary young men with extraordinarily big dreams.

Reading between the lines, it would be easy to assume that Marcus was a third young man with equally big dreams, but the career that follows belies that hypothesis.

After graduating, Marcus and Toby headed to California. But where Toby used seed money from Gladiator Inc's young CEO, Ben Russo, to start his own company, Marcus got a job as a software engineer.

A regular job.

Because Marcus Dane, best friend to billionaires, was a regular Joe—hypothesis number two.

But after a few years of chasing the tech 401k dream, he walked away from the suburban house and workplace-with-a-gym-and-smoothie-bar, for...

I glance around me.

Nothing, really.

Maybe everything.

Trees. Fresh air.

Painfully high altitude that sort of makes me faint, although that could also be attributed to the clash of wills with the bearded mountain man.

Freedom.

Hypothesis number three, should anyone still care about Marcus Dane after he disappeared up a mountain, is that he's seen the inside workings of capitalist, tech-worshiping America, and he doesn't like it. In fact, he hates it, and now that society has broken down to the point of chaos, he's going to use whatever platform he can find to ensure the things that really matter to him—the environment, protection of the land and animals, water—have a voice.

No matter what official edict gets handed down from on high, Mr. Alt Park Service won't be silenced.

As far as I know, nobody has looked at Marcus Dane but me. I've run the story in the loosest of terms past two of my favorite editors. Both were open to hearing more, but I needed to put this trip on my credit card because nobody is paying freelancers to hunt stories like this. Not in the heat of summer. Not when there are courthouses and law offices to stalk.

If I wanted to pay the rent, I'd join the stringers from MSNBC and CNN outside the Washington DC law firms and wait for the White House staffers to come to me. Most of them are a sympathetic look away from spilling their guts over coffee.

Except...

I want to pay my rent, but not by lunging desperately at low-hanging fruit.

I want to write a good story. Something I had to dig for, that nobody else has any idea about yet.

I want to expose a real truth, which is getting harder and harder to do these days.

If I do that, I'll be able to land a job that pays the rent on a regular basis.

Teach a man to fish, they say.

Or in 2017...teach a woman to follow a wild hunch, no matter how high up a mountain it drags her.

CHAPTER THREE

MARCUS

I TIP my cup against my lower lip, but it's empty now. I'd forgotten that as I sat and stewed over the fact she's still outside.

Well, coffee break is over.

I pick up my phone and scroll through the search results that came up when I typed in her name.

Poppy Lisowski is quite the intrepid reporter. I have no doubt she knows everything about me. Where I went to school, who I'm friends with.

What my political affiliation is—registered independent, always have been, always will be—and how I like my pizza.

Extra pepperoni, green peppers, and onions. Always have, always will.

The thing about me that Poppy Lisowski doesn't know is that those two things are equally weighted in my world, but I'm not sure I want to tell her that just yet.

I'm not sure I want her to go away.

I lift my cup again before remembering...

Ah, hell.

Duty calls.

I stalk to the door and swing it open. "I need to head out to check some day site permits. You want to come with me, Reporter Girl?"

Her back stiffens for a micro-second, then she scrambles to her feet. "Sure thing, Ranger Boy."

I force myself to keep walking and not stop and give her a reaction to that. But I see her, and hear her.

I'll only call her a girl again when I want to get a reaction.

A better man would take the warning completely and not do it at all, but where's the fun in that?

We've got a three-hour slow climb up and down mountainsides in my truck ahead of us. We're going to need to have a little fun.

"Where is the campground?" she asks as I steer down the lane toward the road that will take us back to the highway.

"Which campground?"

"The one with the day permits you're checking?" She pulls a notebook out of her bag, and then the recorder is back, too.

I glance at it. "Do you want to get the spelling and everything just right for your story?"

She ignores the barb and waits for me to answer.

I don't.

"I'd like to return to the question about your friendships with Toby Hunt and Ben Russo."

Ah. Now she's dragging Ben into this. I grunt.

"Mr. Hunt and Mr. Russo haven't always seen eye-to-eye on political issues..."

Now it's my turn to wait, but she doesn't finish the rest of that thought. "Is that a question?"

Because if it is, she's wrong. I don't spend a lot of time thinking about the political contributions my friends make, but I know enough about their business interests and their personal realities to know that whatever money they donate, wherever they donate it, that's no reflection on anything.

Not much of a reflection, anyway.

Fuck, I hate this shit.

"Are you aware—"

"No."

"You didn't let me ask the question."

"Doesn't matter. The answer is always going to be no. On the record. No, I'm not aware. No, I can't comment on my friends' lives. No, I haven't discussed whatever it is you're asking about with them. No, no, no."

"Are you aware that Toby Hunt's company is working on a double-encrypted Bluetooth solid state memory device that can invisibly run in the background of a mobile phone? It will, apparently, mask the connection once it's made. And apps can be installed on the device instead of the phone, making them invisible, too."

"That sounds complicated."

"Is that a no, you aren't aware?"

I can't answer that question. Might be time to break out another Reporter Girl comment.

But that makes me think about how her mouth pursed when I did it before, and that feels a little close to tugging on a girl's pigtails because I like it.

If I want to see her soft lips pull together like that again, I can find an up-front way to make that happen.

We still have hours together, after all.

Plenty of time to explore why I'm drawn to her, even while she's grilling me on shit I know nothing about—and some shit I know plenty about, but won't tell her.

Ever.

That's just how friendships go. I'm a vault.

"Are you aware that your newspaper is owned by a ruthless billionaire who doesn't think twice about putting competitors out of business to chomp up market share?"

"I'm not actually employed by any single publication, so it's not *my* newspaper. Are you aware that the blog I also write for regularly covers that sort of thing quite critically?"

No, I've never read the blog that was on her business card, but I sure as shit will look it up tonight. "What exactly is your goal here?"

"You didn't answer my question about the campground. How far is it?"

"I said I needed to check day site permits. Plural." The truck bounces over a rut in the road, and she gasps. I keep going. "And then you pulled out your recorder, like I'm going to say something that might score you a Pulitzer Prize. So I didn't answer your question, but I will now. We're not going to 'a campground', exactly. I'm doing my daily loop of a number of day site permit locations."

She stiffens on the passenger seat, and despite my best efforts to glare straight ahead, I see her out of the corner of my eye. I see her glance down at her recorder, and turn it off. I see her jaw tighten, then relax, and I see her sigh and turn to look out the window.

I see her cross her legs, flashing me another few inches of soft thigh.

Damn it. Now my jaw is tight, too.

That's not to say I don't like it. I do, but it's a performance.

A trick.

If a woman is going to slide her skirt up her thighs for me, it's gotta be because she wants me to chase the hem with my tongue. Because she wants to get lost for a few hours, and part company with a mutually fond memory.

Not because she thinks I can be distracted by my dick.

She taps her fingers on her knee, then sighs and lifts her hand to her mouth. Her lips part, pink and shiny, and she sinks her perfect white teeth into the fleshy pad of her thumb.

This was a mistake. I can't drag her around the park with me. Another few hours of this antagonism and who the hell knows what will happen?

Maybe you can chase her through the forest and convince her to let you peek up her skirt.

Not happening.

I slam on the brakes and jerk the truck off the path. She scrambles to hang on to her recorder, her skirt, her plan of seduction.

I don't care. I point to her door. "Get out."

"Excuse me?" She spins around, looking back up the road.

Yeah, we're a few miles from where she left her car.

Not my problem.

"Get. Out."

"You get out," she says hotly.

Fine.

I leap out the driver's side and stalk around to her door.

More thigh greets me as she holds up her hand—clearly, she's figured out I'm serious, and she doesn't want me to touch her.

Fine by me. I don't want to touch her either. Not much, anyway. Definitely not in anger.

I actually want to touch her way too much for a stranger who's poking around my life.

I step back and cross my arms over my chest. "What are you playing at?"

She slithers to the ground and straightens her dress. "Nothing."

"With your little display in the truck."

"What display?"

"Letting your skirt ride up. Biting your thumb. Turning off the recorder."

Her eyes go wide as I list what she did. She stares at me, stock-still, then gasps again and shoves her hands hard against my chest. "You... you... you..."

I step back, and she shoves me again.

"You... beast!" She laughs, and shakes her head, but when her gaze collides with mine, there's no humor there. Just angry, pissed-off woman. "Okay, let's start at the top. I'm wearing a skirt. Yes. I have legs, that's a fun fact, too. And you saw part of them. Whoop-di-fucking-doo, Ranger Boy. Second, if I was biting my thumb, it was to keep from criticizing your reckless fucking driving. And finally, I turned off my recorder because this interview is a waste of my fucking time. And if you think for a hot second that I might use my feminine wiles to get a story out of you, you're a fucking asshole who deserves to be hunted down by paparazzi. I'll make sure that happens just as soon as I get off this fucking godforsaken mountain."

"You're going to give up, just like that?" I move forward again, crowding into her personal space. "Lose your story?"

"There's no story here," she spits, her jaw set and her eyes glittering. "Not one worth writing."

"Because I barked at you?"

"Because you leered at me."

I had done that. Twice. Maybe three times. And I'd done it mostly to scare her away, but also a little bit because she itched at me. That itch now flares up, hot and red and annoyingly principled. "I was trying to scare you off."

She laughs again without humor. "It worked, you pervert. How the fuck am I supposed to get back to my car now? Because I'm sure as hell not getting back in your truck."

CHAPTER FOUR

POPPY

"GET BACK IN MY TRUCK? I just told you to get out of it." His nostrils flare as he glares at me.

Makes sense. I did call him a pervert. It was never explicitly covered in my journalism classes, but calling an interview subject a pervert is definitely a bad idea.

But he read something filthy into me biting my thumb. Into how I wear a skirt. And that was before I called him names. "For some made-up reasons that hide the fact you're really uncomfortable about me sniffing around." I fumble for my recorder and turn it back on. "Change of plans, buster. Your story is once again *super fascinating.*"

He growls under his breath, something I don't catch, and he plants his hands on his lean, tight hips. He needs to stop doing that. It's distracting.

He stares at the sky. Finally, he shakes his head and looks

right at me. "It's a gorgeous day, ma'am. Enjoy your hike back to where you parked your car."

And then he gets in his truck and *drives away*.

I watch the cloud of dust he leaves behind fade, then turn around.

Of course he's not wrong. It is a beautiful day. And it only takes me an hour to get back to my car, in which time I come up with a fabulous new angle for my story.

I dig into my suitcase for a pair of jeans, which I wiggle into right there in front of Ranger Boy's cabin, hiking them up under my skirt.

Screw him and his pervy looks at my legs.

Then I haul out my computer and sit on the porch.

It takes him three hours to return.

In that time, I write a first draft of a piece that's pretty damn good, if I do say so myself.

He takes his time opening the truck door. It creaks, slowly, then his boots land on the ground with a heavy thud.

"I thought you were leaving." He says it like a statement. A dry observation, not letting on if he's surprised or not.

Well, tough titties for him, it's a free country. "I have a day pass for the park," I say without looking up. "It's been quite inspirational for my writing."

"Writing about me?"

I take a deep breath. "If I say yes, will you comment on the record?"

He sighs. "Sure."

"Will they be helpful comments?"

"Now you're asking a lot." He laughs, which surprises *me*, and I jerk my head up. He's half-smiling at me. The other half of his face is still tense and frown-y. It's not the worst look for him. "But as you just reminded me, it's still a free country, so they'll be whatever they'll be. The truth, I can promise you that."

I turn on my recorder and hold it out, my hand steady and sure. "You're a strong believer in the truth, aren't you, Mr. Dane?"

"Only way to live."

"How does that balance with someone's right to privacy?"

He scowls. "My privacy?"

"Anyone's. A secret service agent who doesn't agree politically with the politician he's tasked with protecting. A Justice Department attorney who needs to write a brief at the request of a racist or a hypocrite. How far should we dig to understand the context around their disagreement?"

"You don't have to dig at all. That's the wrong context in which to frame questions of morality or constitutionality."

"What's the proper context?"

"We have a guiding set of principles in this country. They're not carved in stone. We've amended them many times. But as they stand, those are our guiding principles and it is against those that we need to measure...whatever you want to question. Policy, law, matters of common practice."

"You're a constitutionalist." I'm surprised, although I don't know why. It makes sense given the rest of the profile I've assembled on him. I was just so focused on him being a part of the resistance that it didn't occur to me that he might also be a conservative.

He gives me an inscrutable look. "No, Ms. Lisowski. I'm a park ranger."

"And do you believe, as a park ranger, you're being asked to do anything unconstitutional right now?"

"Right now? In this moment? If anything, it's quite the opposite." He grins again. "As a representative of the government, I wouldn't want to do anything to abridge the freedom of the press."

That wasn't what I'd just asked him, and he knows it. I'm also not impressed by his easy recital of a few words from the Constitution.

I am not.

Definitely not aroused by the grin and the beard and the sharp-minded mountain man aesthetic.

"That's a lot of fancy talk to obscure the fact you haven't really answered the question."

He nods, acknowledging my point. Then he points to the cabin. "I'm hungry. Are you hungry?"

No, I'm hot on a story. I'll eat when it's done. But then I remember his change of heart with regard to answering questions. We can meet in the middle. "Sure."

He leads me inside, and I tuck my computer away, but I keep my recorder out this time.

"I've got some sandwiches. Do you have any weird food things?"

I roll my eyes at the way he phrased it, but don't allow him to goad me into reframing that. Big picture, Poppy. He's talking to you again. "I'll eat whatever."

He pulls an insulated lunch bag from under his desk, and a big thermos. He has a mug out for himself already and he stalks to a cupboard on the wall, where he finds another one for me.

Ceramic coated metal, straight out of a lumberjack fantasy. "Can I take some pictures?"

"Knock yourself out."

I mostly take pictures of the lunch he spreads out for us, but I also make sure I get shots of his smart phone sitting on the edge of the desk, next to a wide ceramic bowl filled with National Park Service keychains. In the background, there's a bulletin board covered in memos. They're probably totally innocuous, but just in case...snapped.

"These two are roast beef, and those are tomato and cheese." He points to a brown paper bag. "Chocolate chip cookies in there."

"No shiny red apple?"

He grins. "Already had it for my snack this morning."

I take a tomato sandwich and sit back, watching him as he digs in. "Do you usually eat lunch so late in the afternoon?"

"Sure. Sometimes."

"How much longer is your work day?"

"A few more hours."

"That's vague."

"You deserve the truth. Nobody said it had to be precise." He says it straight, but then the corners of his mouth twitch up.

"Ooh, Ranger Boy made a funny."

He lifts one shoulder. "Maybe. I..." He glances at a piece of paper on his desk. "One of the permits is until six, so I'll want to check that site to make sure they've cleared out. I'll be done after that." He lifts his gaze to meet mine. "Why? Want to take me out for dinner?"

That's an excellent idea. "Yes. But I should warn you, I'm on a tight budget, so it might be sandwiches again."

"Your fancy newspapers don't have a budget for wining and dining reluctant subjects?"

It's none of his business that I'm doing this freelance. "I doubt our readers would appreciate if they did."

"Fair point." He pops the last bite of his sandwich into his mouth, then reaches for the cookies. "Would you like one?"

"Did you bake them yourself?"

He shakes his head. "Made by pros at a bakery in town."

I consider the offer carefully, and then lean forward—but he pulls the bag back. "Hey."

"Tell me your story first." He gives me a no-nonsense look that works.

I sigh. "Fine. I think you've seen the inside workings of capitalist, tech-worshiping America, and you don't like it. You left that behind for something...purer. National service. And for the last eight years, you've done your part here. Working with those constructs of freedom and access for everyone. But now society has broken down to the point of chaos, so you're going to use whatever platform you can to shine a light on the darkness that's threatening..." I wave my hands. "This."

"There's just one problem with your theory."

"What's that?"

"When have I ever shown any interest in shining a spotlight on anything?"

There was that. "Desperate times call for desperate measures."

"Are we in desperate times, Poppy?" Now he's playing with me again, but I don't miss the edge in his voice.

I square my shoulders and nod. "Yes. Do you know what I did last week? I took a self-defense for front-line journalists workshop. Not just any old self-defense workshop—one specifically for front-line journalists. And it was sold out. They're running the same workshop three times a week in Washington right now."

His eyes glitter. "And still you come here in pursuit of a story."

"Yes."

He swears under his breath and picks up his phone. He looks at it long and hard, then swings his gaze back to me. "We can talk more over dinner."

The dismissal is clear. I nod. "Thank you."

I stand up and tell him the name of the hotel where I'm staying in nearby Rifle.

His eyes are still hard as he nods. "I'll meet you up there at seven."

CHAPTER FIVE

MARCUS

I'M STILL NOT sure how I ended up standing outside Poppy's hotel room wearing a buttoned-down shirt. She called me a pervert. I kicked her out of my truck.

But then she waited me out, put on jeans—yes, I noticed—and chowed down on my tomato and cheddar sandwiches while she revealed that she could see right to my soul.

She might be magic.

She definitely deserves an interview.

And I'm not done with her in all the other ways she occupies my brain, too.

Add in the disturbing but not surprising fact she needs to take self-defense workshops just to do her damn job, and I'm definitely in a weird state. The thought of anyone hurting her for asking questions makes me see red.

I knock again, since she didn't answer the first time, and the door swings open on the third rap.

She's breathless, and her hair swings loose around her shoulders. "Hi," she says, waving me in. "I'm running a little late. Was writing. Just getting changed now."

I try to tell my dick not to take that the wrong way, but it's too late.

She's decent—she's wearing another dress, this one longer than the one that drove me to distraction, and it's zipped up and everything.

Still drives me to distraction. And it's only almost zipped up.

As she spins around in a slow circle, looking for...something...I notice that the top inch of her zipper—the part that would be hard for her to reach on her own—is gaping open.

My fingers itch to fix that for her.

Maybe she'll ask.

And maybe you'll be appointed the next Secretary of the Interior.

That thought does a good job of killing my boner. Fuck.

"Can we walk somewhere from here?" Poppy asks, interrupting my internal rant. She's holding up two different shoes, one with a heel, the other without.

She came to Colorado with at least three pairs of shoes, none of them really appropriate for the mountains.

And I don't care, not even a little bit. "Yeah, we can walk, if you'd like. But I can drive us somewhere if you want to wear the other ones."

She gives me a sly smile. "That was a trick question, Ranger Boy. I'm not risking being stranded somewhere I might need to hike back from again. Flats it is."

I wince. "Right. I apologize for that. And I promise it won't happen again."

She laughs. "I'm going to hold you to that promise, but honestly, the walk was good. Churned my story around in my head, didn't it?"

She grabs her bag and slings it across her body.

"Your...um..." I move closer, my fingers reaching out. "Zipper."

She turns again in a slow circle, and stops with her back to me. "Is it down a little?"

"Yeah. I could—" I cut myself off as she reaches behind her and fixes it. "You're good."

"Thanks."

Here's the thing. I'm a man of a decent amount of experience with women. So there's no reason why it should surprise me that she's blushing as she turns around. That I'm feeling weird in my chest, like that blush is a gift she's giving me.

Furthermore, I'm a grown-up who knows that sometimes, often, jobs come before lust. And I haven't forgotten she's here to do a job. That I was doing my job, earlier, when I shut her down—or when I relented and gave her access again.

She's working here, in Colorado.

But she's not working here, in this room. I suddenly know this as an absolute truth. I know this as a man, and I realize...this is one of those rare times when lust comes before the job, when it's worth risking everything for a taste.

This woman wants to expose me as something I'm not, and in the process might expose things that I am, of which she—and the rest of the world—are currently unaware. I shouldn't be attracted to her.

And yet I am.

I should be wary. I should misdirect her.

But if I want a taste...

Fuck. My noble sensibilities will be the death of me. "We probably should talk," I finally say. That's the truth.

"Can we do that after dinner?" She gives me an earnest look, and I choose to read it as, *don't do this. Don't say that we can't...eat, flirt, look, want, yearn.* And since that's all I'm choosing to read it as—no mention of touching, kissing, tasting, taking—then we're fine.

"Yeah."

Her earnest expression lights up with another sly smile. Curious, confident, and committed—to both getting her story, and God willing, getting her man. Or at least I can dream. And she stokes that fantasy, too, maybe unwittingly. Her eyes soften. "We'll get there, Marcus."

CHAPTER SIX

POPPY

I'M NOT sure when the day shifted, but at some point, I went from warily thinking that Marcus was definitely a creepy pervert, to cautiously hoping he might be a delightful pervert—a thought which shocks the heck out of me.

There's no room in this trip for delightful anything, so I really need to shut down the flirting.

Do I shut it down, though? Nope. I promise we can resume it later. What the eff, Poppy?

I can't help it. After five years of being hit on by lobbyists, Hill staffers, and military men temporarily stationed in the Washington area—all of them looking for a sloppy blowjob, only some eager to reciprocate, and none promising a call the next day—it's kind of nice to do this weird tug-of-war thing with Marcus.

There still wouldn't be a call tomorrow.

And there won't be any sloppy anythings tonight.

Instead, we've got this weird, simmering tension, and it's kind of fun.

I shouldn't trust him.

I don't know him.

I'm writing a story about him...

And yet right now, all I can think about is the look in his eyes when he reached for my zipper. And in that second, I wanted him to tug it down, not up, and I needed to straighten it myself, because if he'd touched me, we wouldn't be heading out the door right now.

Thankfully he can't read my thoughts, and instead of stripping me naked, he leads me out of the hotel and down the street. "We've got a bunch of options. Pizza, subs, a sports bar that does a half-assed attempt at being a saloon. Thai, BBQ, a couple of Mexican places..."

"Which is your favorite?"

He shrugs. "BBQ, probably."

"Then lead the way."

The sun is low in the sky to our west, and I can't help but notice—again—how beautiful it is here. I tell Marcus as much, and he gives me a slow, easy grin. "Why do you think I moved here?"

"You like it better than California?"

He nods. "Most of the time. I miss surfing, but I only managed to do that once or twice a year. Here I get out climbing almost every week. You know, when I worked at SwiftEx as a software engineer, they talked a good game about work-life balance. Mostly because our campus was in the heart of Silicon Valley and their competitors were doing the same thing. But I still worked a ninety-hour work week. I was on call a lot, had long days. Here..."

He turned in a slow circle, holding out his arms.

"You worked a long day today, though."

He starts walking again. "Doesn't feel like it."

"How many of those shifts do you work in a week?"

"Who's asking? Reporter Girl?" He says it deliberately, slowly, and he watches me for a reaction.

I don't give him one. It doesn't rile me up tonight, and the other reaction is inappropriate. "Yes. I'm asking on the record."

"Usually four. Sometimes five if I'm swapping with someone."

"And this week?"

"No comment."

"Really?" I hustle to get in front of him and we both stop. "Why no comment?"

"No comment to that, too."

"Is the communications ban still in effect?"

He gives me a wry half-smile. "No comment."

"And off the record?"

He steps around me. "Let's get some food first."

The BBQ place is a walk-up counter in a strip mall, but it smells amazing, and there are a couple of small tables covered in plastic clothes. We place our orders, then I grab a table while Marcus buses our food over.

"Ask me what I was doing this time last year," he finally says, after I've watched him lick sauce off his thumb a few times too many.

That shouldn't be hot.

There's something seriously weird about the Colorado air.

Maybe it's that there just isn't enough of it at this altitude. I'm lightheaded and hallucinating. Wait, that was a clue. "Ask you... Okay. What were you doing this time last summer?"

His mouth tightens as he leans back in his chair. "Not checking day site permits."

"Who did that?"

"Seasonal staff. Mostly students."

That's been covered reasonably well in the press, although I make a mental note to layer it into my story, too. The impact of the hiring ban is widespread. "Mostly? Who else gets hired as a seasonal employee?"

He glances out the window. "Locals."

That twigs something for me that the Alt Park Service Twitter handle re-tweeted the week before. Local economies tanking because of cutbacks in federal programs. "Not enough people talk about that impact."

He shakes his head. "Nope."

"Do you? Maybe secretly?"

He laughs and shakes his head. "On Twitter? Let me ask you this. Where would I get the time or information, when I spend all day on a mountain?"

Truthfully, my story had diverged from that lede over the afternoon. "My personal research shows you get excellent reception at that cabin."

"That's not your story, is it?" His jaw flexes, then flares as he grits his teeth. "I thought..."

"What kind of journalist would I be if I let my attraction to you cloud..."

His dark eyes glitter as he stares across the table at me.

Well, that was a dumb thing to confess. I drop my gaze to

the leftovers I couldn't finish—not because they weren't delicious, but because the portions were insane. Now I've blown both my interview and what might have been the oddest first date ever.

Quality reporting, quality peopling, Poppy. "I apologize," I say, still staring into the small dish of baked beans. "Let me backtrack."

"No." His hands appear in my field of vision, and he grabs my basket of food. "I think we're done here."

I stand as he dumps our baskets on the counter, gives a curt "thanks" to the people in the kitchen, and pushes his way out the front doors.

I'm *so* glad I picked the flats.

It takes some good jogging to catch up, because his legs are long and his stride is fierce. "Marcus..."

"You should probably go back to calling me Mr. Dane," he bites out when I finally get in front of him.

I put my hands on my hips. "I don't think that will make a difference, do you?"

He glares down at me. Then he looks around, swearing under his breath. Finally, he looks back at me. "I'm going to kiss you."

"What?"

"Fair warning."

"I...uh...okay—" No sooner does the last word jerk out of my mouth than his lips are on mine, his hands in my hair, and there's a hungry desperation in the embrace.

Like he knows this is a terrible idea.

Terribly good.

Terribly confusing.

Terribly...nice.

Oh.

His lips soften as I kiss him back, because fuck it, I've already screwed the interview. I might as well save the connection.

So what if he's a secret Twitter resistance fighter? I can find another story to write.

"I'm not your Twitter guy," he growls.

"Stop reading my mind."

"Is that what you were just thinking about?" He brushes his lips against mine. "I clearly wasn't doing my job, then."

"I was..." I exhale as I push up on my toes. "It doesn't matter."

He kisses me again, deeper this time. I'm totally ready for him to get handsy, too, but no such luck.

Instead, he eases back and gives me an unexpectedly tender smile. "This is not how I expected my day to go when I woke up."

"That makes two of us." I bite the corner of my lip.

"I'm really not the guy you're looking for," he says softly. "I should have been straight up with you about that earlier. I probably agree with him, whoever he is. But I'd also bet ten bucks he's not actually a park ranger."

"He, or she, gets an awful lot right. One of the tech reporters did an analysis of all the active alt twitter accounts, and the Alt Park Service account—"

Marcus holds up his hands. "And if I wanted to, I could run you an alternate analysis that showed that account to be following the news, not making it. But I don't, because it doesn't matter. There's a resistance movement online, and there are real people behind it. Sure. But the people are almost certainly not who they are pretending to be."

"I know that."

"Then why are you here?"

"Because you're a fascinating guy," I blurt out. And it's true. He's the reason I'm here. Ever since I read his bio—

Damn it. I repeat the curse out loud, then I stop my feet and spin away from him. "Holy crap, how could I be so stupid?" I'm burning up inside as I move toward my hotel, my legs whipping beneath me. Faster, faster.

This time, it's Marcus calling *my* name, Marcus getting in front of me and setting his hands on my shoulders. "Poppy, what the hell just happened?"

"I flew all the way out here because I have a crush on you!" I yell in his face. "Which is the worst kind of journalism ever, by the way. And I'm smarter than that. I blew you up in my head to be some kind of hero of the people, and I was so focused on being right about that, I didn't see that I was distracted by your...your..."

He gives me a wary look, his eyebrows raised. "My... what?"

"Mountain man appeal," I mutter.

He grins. "Ah."

"Shut up."

"That's nice courting language," he says, chuckling as I glower at him. "But I can see why you're frustrated."

"Good. Now if you'll just let me head back to my hotel..."

"But you have a crush on me," he says, stepping aside.

"Had."

"No, you said have. Present tense. Active crush."

"It's the thin air up here, it makes people crazy."

"You said the crush started in Washington. Thick air there."

"Different kind of crazy. There may have been a moment flying over Kansas City where I had a chance to see this situation objectively, but I missed it."

"I have a crush on you, too."

"You just met me."

"Insta-crush."

I give him a sideways look of disbelief. Kissing aside, I don't believe Marcus does insta-anything. "You kicked me out of your truck."

"That was self-preservation. I wanted you something fierce, and I thought you were toying with my sensitive emotions."

"I wasn't."

"I know."

"You wanted me, even in the truck?"

"I wanted you from the first second I saw you. Ponytail and wedge sandals and determined expression. I dug it all."

Ugh. "That makes this even worse."

"Why?"

"I put this flight on my credit card. I need to turn in a story that'll justify the expense."

"So why can't you turn in the story that had you glowing earlier?"

"Because it was an infatuation piece! It's not good journalism! It's fawning over the hard-done-by park ranger."

"That sounds great." He clears his throat when I shook him another side-eye. "Or not. Okay. I can see the conflict of interest."

I groan.

"Then we'll get you a new story," he says. "One that has nothing to do with me. What time is your flight back?"

"Tomorrow evening."

"Okay. I'm on it."

"You don't need to—"

He holds up his hand. "Maybe not. But I'm going to, anyway. Consider it my penance for the accidental luring with my mountain man appeal."

He's enjoying that way too much. I *should* let him help me as punishment. "Deal."

CHAPTER SEVEN

POPPY

A HEARTY KNOCK at my hotel room door wakes me up the next morning.

I stumble out of bed, bleary-eyed and quite confused about why my delicious dream about kissing a man with a beard ended so abruptly. Turning in a circle, I take in a bunch of facts at the same time.

It's barely light out, for one.

And the knocking sounds happy, for another.

Okay, that's just two facts.

"What is it?" I ask, my brain still fuzzy as I pull the door open.

Marcus holds up a thermos of coffee and gives me a grin.

A bearded grin.

And it all comes rushing back. The kissing, the yelling, the admission of a crush.

His crazy plan that he'll just find me another story.

"What time is it?"

He slides his gaze down my body, then back up again. "I really like the tiny pajamas. It's almost six."

"Almost six. Like...the wrong side of six?"

"What kind of reporter are you that you don't wake up at dawn?"

The kind who stays up past midnight re-working her story so it doesn't sound quite so much like a love letter to a certain khaki uniform. I don't bother answering him. "Is that coffee for me?"

He hands it over and invites himself inside. I don't mind, because he's in his uniform and that's delicious. So is the coffee.

"I've got a name for you," he says, handing over a piece of paper. "Guy by the name of Kaden. He's a volunteer firefighter, and an experienced climber. We've hired him as a seasonal worker for the last eight years. This year, no go. He's got a good story."

"Thank you."

"He's climbing today. I thought I could take you out there. Good photo opportunity."

"Okay."

"I want to kiss you again."

I jerk my head up from examining his neat, square handwriting. "What?"

He said it in the same way he'd told me about his friend. Now he says it again, but there's a vibration to his tone. An urgency. "I want to kiss you again. I want a hell of a lot more than that, too. I wasn't sure if I should kiss you good morning, or—"

I set down the thermos, my hands shaking. "Yes."

He's across the room in two strides, and he doesn't just kiss me. He lifts me up, his hands strong and sure on my torso.

"I don't want to complicate anything," he murmurs against my lips.

I smile. "Complicate away."

His kiss is confident and sure. Firm lips and a light tongue, just a tease at the seam of my mouth, then sweet, exploratory licks when I open for him. He kisses like he works—methodically, with an edge of promised danger.

Always in control, I bet.

I want to mess him up. I want to make him growl. Would he? What sounds would he make if I licked my way down his corded throat and tasted the skin at the edge of his uniform collar?

Before I get a chance to find out, he sets me down. His eyes are dark and serious as he steps back. "Good morning."

I cross my arms over my chest. Not now, nipples. Later. "Good morning."

"I should let you get dressed." He clears his throat, and jerks his thumb over his shoulder. "I'll wait in the hallway."

"Five minutes," I say breathlessly.

Once he's outside, I look at the name and phone number in my hand. Climbers. Okay.

From my suitcase, I pull my jeans, and a long-sleeved t-shirt, and after I get dressed, I tug on my running shoes and brush my hair back into a ponytail.

I find Marcus in the hallway, scrolling through his phone. He tucks it away and stands up, giving me a once-over that lingers on my shoes. "So you do own sensible footwear."

"Of course I do."

"Those are the fourth pair of shoes I've seen you in, and the first that are appropriate for the mountains."

I grin. He's counting my shoes. That's adorable. "But these look ridiculous with a dress. And I love dresses. You see the bind I'm in."

He hesitates. "Fair point."

I bump my shoulder against his arm as we walk down the hallway. "But I'm glad you approve of my footwear choice today."

He doesn't say anything, but the side of his mouth twitches up into a smile.

As he opens his truck door for me, he sets his hand in the small of my back and leans in, pressing his lips against my temple. "I love your dresses, too."

I finish drinking the coffee he brought me and catalog my thoughts about everything that has happened over the last twenty hours while he drives me out to a popular climbing spot.

"Don't blast this kid with a lot of questions."

"I won't." I'm not sure what the angle is on this story, but it's not deep investigative anything, I'm sure of that. I'm not even sure I can sell it, but something is better than nothing. "I'll be kind."

"Just be yourself. That goes a long way out here. And..." He gives me a sideways glance. "You do that well. I'm not trying to tell you how to be. Promise."

I take a deep breath. "I appreciate it."

"It'll help that I'm dropping you off."

I nod.

"And I'll be back in a few hours."

I'm pretty sure he's set this up deliberately, so I need to take my time or spend a few hours sitting in the dust all by myself. But it'll take me that long to get a good story anyway, so I'm not complaining.

As promised, Kaden is waiting for us there. He looks wary of me—a look I'm starting to get used to—but Marcus introduces us and smooths out the introduction.

We stick to climbing talk for the first hour. He takes me to a spot where people are taking turns doing quick ascents, and when it's his turn, his friends are happy to chat with me, too.

"How many of you have previously worked for the National Park Service?" I ask.

Half of them put up their hands.

"So what are you doing this year?"

Two of them don't have regular work lined up. Others are working in restaurants or for private outfitters.

Kaden comes back and sits down just as one of his friends finishes a rant. He scrubs his hand over his face. "Tell me about it."

"How about you, Kaden?" I turn my recorder in his direction.

He screws up his face and shakes his head. "I don't have a job yet. Doing this, living in my van. I'll pick up more hours in the fall when I go back to school. And my girlfriend's pretty understanding."

"Brianne was one of the lucky ones," another climber says.

"My girlfriend got hired on early this year," Kaden explains. "She's one of the few who started work in January and so far, hasn't been let go. But that's precarious, too, you know?"

I nod. "So this has affected your entire community."

"For sure. Even those that have jobs this summer, like Brianne—she's stressed. I'm telling you, you want to see the next generation of political outrage? That's my girlfriend right there. She's *pissed*. And with good reason."

"Yeah, she's on Twitter all the time, isn't she?" another climber asks.

I didn't get that guy's name, and I suddenly, blindingly, realize it doesn't matter.

Brianne. Someone on the inside, fired up, but in real danger of losing her job.

Someone who might not know enough about technology to not leave a few breadcrumbs for a reporter.

A young person who a good guy might feel protective of.

I ask a few more questions, take a few more pictures, but my brain is now officially occupied with a different story altogether.

When Marcus comes to pick me up, I wait until we're back at the hotel to ask him the opening question I've decided on. I'm not going to beat around the bush. After what we've shared, that wouldn't be fair.

He comes out around to my side of his truck to help me out, but I hop down on my own and pace away from him. When I turn back, he's giving me a wary look. Good. He should have some warning that this is coming. "Do you have one of Toby Hunt's masking devices?"

"No," he says carefully.

"Did you?" My pulse hammers in my neck. "At one point? And maybe you gave it to someone else? Someone who couldn't carry two cell phones on her without being too obvious?"

His face tightens up. "What are you talking about?"

"Someone named Brianne?"

"How the hell—"

"She's dating that climber. Kaden. Good kid. But he doesn't know what his girlfriend is up to."

"And neither do you. Neither do I, frankly." But his tone changed on the last point. Like he only didn't know the whole picture because maybe he was deliberately keeping himself in the dark—now.

"I bet if I go through the followers for Alt Nat Park Service, I'll find a relatively anonymous account in the early follows. Someone who doesn't participate on Twitter a lot, someone who sits back and watches what's being said—particularly about his own corner of the country."

"Don't write that."

"I can't—"

"Write about *anything* else."

"That's not how this works. I'm not going to kill a story that is worth writing."

He gives me a thunderous look of disapproval, and I realize too late, he's not talking about himself. "She'll be fired."

I press my lips together and think. I could change the details. Mask her identity. Maybe...

"For God's sake, Poppy, put yourself in her shoes. Insert yourself into this situation for one God damned minute and stop pretending it's just another *fucking story*. You have to take self-defense courses! This is not normal. This is fucked up. And she doesn't deserve to be punished for, as you said, shining a spotlight on the reality of decisions made a world away from us."

He's right. I know it. But there was something else in his diatribe... "Insert myself."

"That's what I just said."

"Right..." I stare off into the distance.

"Poppy?"

"Hang on a second." I pace back and forth, then ball my hands into fists. Gah, it's so close. But how do I do it without...

I turn and I look at him. Oh, he's not going to like this.

"I could do that. I could insert myself into the story. I can change it into a process piece about me. But it would be you, too. You are, after all, quite appealing."

"Quite appealing." He snorts. "I'm going to put that on my resume."

He's joking, but it hurts my chest to think that he might actually need to look for a new job because of me. "I don't want to put you in any kind of danger, though."

He gives me a dark look. Is that better than the thunderous look from before? I feel like it might be, but my brain is spinning. The world is upside down, because I have a story, I have a lead to follow, and I don't want to.

If Marcus says no, I'll find another way. If he—

"Okay."

"Okay?"

"I trust you. Write me into your story. Call me cute. Whatever you gotta do."

"You just met me. How can you trust me?"

He moves closer and cups my face in his hands. "Because of that look on your face right now. You don't want to hurt anyone. I know you don't. And this won't hurt me. It's a good idea." He brushes a kiss across my mouth. "I gotta get back to work. Write like the wind, Reporter Girl."

"Okay, Ranger Boy." I swallow around the lump in my throat. "See you later?"

"Come find me in a couple of hours." He gives me a lopsided grin. "I'll share my second lunch with you."

Lunch. How are we only at the middle of the day?

CHAPTER EIGHT

MARCUS

I'M FOLLOWING up on a report of a bear cub trapped in a dumpster when I get an email from Poppy.

From: Poppy Lisowski
To: Marcus Dane

Okay, here's my article. I guess I'm sending it to you for comment? This is weird. Also, I'm past the point of hangry, so I'm bringing along more food for our lunch.

There's an attachment, but I have a bear cub to reunite with his mother before said mother loses her shit, so I just fire back a quick reply.

From: Marcus Dane
To: Poppy Lisowski

I didn't realize you had my email address. But I look forward to reading the article. Pick up cookies at the bakery.

I leave my phone in the truck and carefully approach the dumpster. Sure enough, there's a small bear inside. "Ah, bud, what have you gotten yourself into?"

I glance around for mama bear, but she's not making herself known just yet. What I need is something long and sturdy to stick into the dumpster to give the adventurous cub a ramp out of his prison. I have a shovel in the back of my truck, and some rescue gear, but none of it is quite long enough, because the big dumpster was recently emptied.

Heading to the edge of the woods, I'm on high alert. If I was mama bear, this is where I'd be. Watching and ready to take out any threat to my baby.

I'm no threat, I projected. Just a friendly ranger, being a good neighbor. I make lots of normal noise as I gather up some downed branches, and keep it up until I get back to the dumpster.

The cub scurries to the far side of the bin as I angle the first branch in. It falls in, not quite tall enough, but the next one is, and so is the third.

I back all the way up to my truck and climb in.

The little fella had a ramp. Now he just had to figure out how to use it.

I read Poppy's article while I waited. By the time I'm nearly to the end of the surprisingly raw, emotional piece about how journalism is shifting beneath her feet, a little black head appears at the mouth of the dumpster. He scrambles up onto the lid, then pulls himself onto the outbuilding before following the slanted roof off in the other direction.

As he disappears, I turn back to Poppy's last two paragraphs.

I flew to Colorado in search of answers. It turned out, I didn't understand the questions. As journalists, we're used to piecing together narratives—for our own stories, and as a community. We lay our articles side-by-side and through that collective lens, we see the bigger picture. The last twenty-four months have cracked that lens. I had to climb a mountain to realize my own focus was zoomed in too tight on entertaining details. I was missing the big picture. I was missing life.

There is a disconnect right now in America. I don't know what questions to ask. But for the next while, I'm going to do more listening than talking (or writing) while I figure it out.

Damn.

I put my truck in drive and head back to my office.

She's sitting on the porch, and she's wearing a dress.

"I thought you were going to write about us," I ask as I hop out of the truck.

"We've only known each other for twenty-four hours. It occurred to me that it was a bit early to know what that *us* might look like, too. More hubris from the journalist."

"You're being too hard on yourself."

"Maybe." She stands up and holds up a familiar brown bag. "I brought you cookies."

"We already have a tradition," I say as I catch her wrist, tugging her and the cookies hard against my chest. "It was a good article."

"Yeah?"

I nod, then I kiss her. Need roars to life inside me in a way I've never experienced before. Sure, I want her. I've wanted her since the first swish of her ponytail yesterday in this very spot. But now I feel something else—a possessive urge to claim her as mine.

It's ridiculous. I'm a lone wolf, always have been. But *always will be* no longer sounds like the right thing to tag on there at the end.

I like this feeling. I like the way she pushes back against my kiss, demanding more. I like the taste of her, the soft sweetness she gives me when I earn it.

"Today was a good day, then?" I run my nose along her cheek as I breathe in the scent of her skin.

"I've salvaged the trip. Professionally, I mean."

"And personally?"

She twists her head and captures my mouth with hers. I get it. I don't want to answer that question, either. Twenty-four hours is hardly enough time to fall in love—especially when a good number of those hours are spent yelling at each other.

"It was more than I could have hoped," she whispers.

That's a damn good answer. I tighten my arms around her and lift. She shrieks and clutches her cookies tight, and I do my damnedest not to notice how her bare legs wrap around my waist.

I carry her inside and set her on my desk, next to my lunch bag.

She crosses her legs and opens the bag of cookies. Her eyes sparkle as she looks up at me. "Hungry?"

"First we eat real food. Then dessert."

She nods solemnly. "Right. Save the sweetness for later."

My cock wants the sweetness right now, and he did not miss the double entendre.

"Soon," I say with a growl, and she grabs the front of my khaki uniform, fisting the fabric as she tugs me in.

"Promise?"

I brace my hands on either side of her. "I want to do a lot of things to you on this desk."

"Any of them inappropriate?"

"All of them."

"I like the sound of that," she whispers, tugging me the last inch so our foreheads bump together. She smiles, her eyes soft. Her breath is warm and sweet against my mouth. "Want to know my secret confession from yesterday?"

"Definitely."

"I was hoping you were a pervert of the highest order."

"You're in luck." I nip at her lower lip, dragging my teeth over her delicate flesh. "Want to know my confession?"

"Yes, please."

Oh, the way she says please. It does wrong, wrong, dirty things to my insides. "I wanted to chase you down. Catch you by the waist and tumble through the grass, until you were straddling me. I wanted you to peel your skirt up and show me what you were wearing underneath."

"That's terrible," she breathes, her eyes big and bright. "I love it."

"We can do that just as soon as we eat. You've had a long morning."

"Okay." She pushes herself off the desk and into my arms.

Goodness like this is what makes people think that things happen for a reason. They don't. That's a lie. Things just happen, randomly and chaotically.

Poppy might think she came here because she had a crush, but that wasn't *me*. She didn't know me yet. She doesn't know me now.

That doesn't stop me from hugging her, though.

Then I clear my throat and she brushes past me to sit in the chair.

I move around my desk, and here we are again. Yesterday, we were adversaries. Today, we share a mutual attraction. That card has been laid on the table.

I pull out the sandwiches and lay them out just so.

Buying time now.

Being a bit of a coward, really.

"It wouldn't be a selfless act," I finally say. I lean back in my chair as Poppy takes a sandwich. "Hypothetically. If I passed on technology to someone who might use it to mask their identity. I wouldn't do that to be a hero."

She lifts one shoulder. "I don't think there are any true heroes now."

How I wish she were wrong. "There are good people putting up a solid fight. It doesn't do anyone any favors to give them superhero capes for doing that, though."

"You're a hard man to figure out, you know that?"

"Normally I would take that as a compliment."

That gets a smile, which I'll take. She takes a bite of her sandwich and points to mine, which remains untouched. I get the message. *Eat.*

Eat, and then we can play.

Her story is done. It wasn't about me. I'm just a guy she met while out here.

No, you're the guy who she's been thinking about for weeks, if not longer.

"Poppy..."

She puts down her sandwich and gives me a half-smile. "Is this where you warn me that we can only be a one-off fling?"

My stomach drops. That wasn't exactly where I was going, but maybe it should be.

"Because I'm fine with that. Crush aside, I'm in a weird place right now. I just emailed in an op-ed proposal when I've never written one of those before, and in it I'm semi-sort-of-maybe saying that I'm stepping aside from journalism for a while. Which is a bold and crazy thing for someone who lives very much month-to-month in a stupidly expensive city to say. So right now is not a great time for me to entertain the notion of a long-distance flirtation, let alone any kind of serious relationship. But I also have some rules about sex and jerks—the two don't work well together for me. So I'm okay with a fling, but it's gotta be honest."

Her voice is tight by the time she finishes saying all of that, and I want to vault over the desk and promise her it won't be like that at all.

Except it probably will.

"I can fly to you," I say.

"What?"

"For our next date. I'll come to you."

"Aren't you working seventy-hour weeks because there aren't enough staff hired on for the summer?"

There is that. I rock my jaw side to side. "Okay, how about this. One of my best friends just got engaged. They're planning a wedding for Thanksgiving, in New York City. Would you like to be my date?"

"You think our second date should be at a wedding four months from now?"

"I wouldn't call it our second date. Maybe fourth or fifth, depending when you fly back, and how many meals we can share between now and then."

"A lot could happen in four months."

Yeah. "Like getting to know each other. Sharing frustrations about how twisted and broken the world is right now."

"I want to do more than be frustrated."

I know. I read her piece. "And that's why you probably won't take a very long break. But I want you to be careful."

She picks up her sandwich again. She chews slowly, her too-clever gaze watching my face. "Hypothetically," she says slowly when she's finished. "Would someone like you be in a position to know something about the dangers of in-depth reporting?"

"Yes." I don't hesitate to answer. I want more than one more afternoon. That's going to require more cards being laid on the table.

"Off the record."

I nod and pick up my phone. I scroll through the most recent updates, and read her a few highlights. I don't look at her as I do it. "Right now there's a nineteen-year-old white supremacist doing background research on every staffer at every major news network that he can find. He's putting them on lists." Rage builds inside me as I read, and I tamp it down. "There's a lot of positive chatter about a beer ad. They're reading a lot of anti-immigration bullshit into it that just doesn't exist. And—" I stop, cutting myself off. She doesn't need to know that there are a group of people joking about killing homeless people.

Jesus Fucking Christ, I hope to God they are joking.

I'm not sure, though. And that's why I keep an eye on them. I'm not alone, either.

Poppy stands and moves around the desk. She puts her hand on my shoulder. "Marcus..."

I pull her into my lap. "You were right. I did figure out who the Alt Park Service account was, and I gave them some pointers for staying under the radar. But that's not the real story. That's a distraction."

She softens, going from perched on my lap to molded against my body in a single, frustrated exhale. "But is writing about the dark underbelly of the internet feeding into that distraction model, too? Is it feeding the trolls? I feel like we need some light to balance the darkness. Don't we?"

If there was an answer to that question, we wouldn't be where we are right now. "I honestly don't know."

"I have to do something." Firm. Resolved. Spirited.

I smile into her hair. "You will."

"I'll be careful."

"Good."

She taps my chest with her fingertips and makes a thinking

sound. "But speaking of not careful...you spend your free time monitoring nihilists and racists in online forums?"

"Everyone needs a hobby."

"I thought yours was rock climbing."

"I do that, too."

"Tell me about it. Off the—"

I cover her mouth with mine. I know it's off the record. I kiss her instead, because that's so much better than the darkness out there. I kiss her because I trust her, because I don't need her assurances.

I just need *her*, for the short time we have left.

I've always taken a pretty pragmatic view of the risks of the world. So why can't I do that when it comes to Poppy?

CHAPTER NINE

POPPY

THERE'S something serious in the way Marcus is holding me. Kissing me.

Serious and a little desperate.

We could get lost in that need, and for a few seconds, I do. I let his kisses consume me, a rolling riptide of sensation.

But we're not going to get to do this again for...four months. And that's if everything goes well. If we continue to like each other, if we keep in touch, if the world doesn't implode...

I trace a finger over his bearded jaw, then let it drop onto his shirt as I peel myself off his body. I really do like his uniform. "So let's count our dates," I murmur as I trace the buttons in a line. "Dinner last night—first date?"

"Not lunch?"

I shake my head. "That was work."

"But dinner..."

It didn't feel like work. "I think from the second you came to my room, that was a date."

His eyes darken. "Agreed. And coffee this morning. Not a great date, but we kissed. That counts."

I smile. "A mini date, and it was fantastic. That's two. And lunch just now was date number three."

"Was?" His lips twist. "Is our date over? Because you're in my lap right now. In my books, that's a good sign for a date progressing."

I sigh regretfully—which takes some serious effort—and press my hand against his chest. "Was. Past tense." I stand up and smooth my hands over my skirt. "If you leave food out on your desk, will the bears break in and destroy your office?"

"I generally try not to leave food out, yes. Why?"

I step back. "No reason. I just thought maybe our next date could start with a chase."

And I turn and sprint for the door.

After I finished writing my story, I took a shower. I shaved my legs. Then I put on a dress, and by some small miracle, I chose my flats.

I hear Marcus behind me. He swears under his breath, then he scrambles to pack up our lunch. That was mean of me. But I'll need the head start, because I don't know where I want him to chase me *to*. I stop at the rise and look left and right. Forest in all directions. It probably doesn't matter.

The door to the little log cabin office thumps open, and I take off again.

I'm at the edge of the forest by the time he catches me. He swings me around, his arms banded about my waist as he hugs me from behind. I laugh as he brings me to the ground in a controlled tackle, then sigh as he rolls onto his back and pulls me, effortlessly, up to straddle his waist.

"Just like this?" I ask as I wiggle against his erection behind me. "This is what you wanted to do to me yesterday?"

He sets his hands on my knees. Warm, calloused fingers stroke my bare skin as he looks up at me with undisguised lust. "Pretty much."

"What else?"

His grin is pure wickedness. "Show me your panties."

I lean just enough to catch the hem of my skirt. Instead of rucking it up my thighs, I lift it into the air.

Beneath me, Marcus shudders.

I'm not wearing any panties.

My cheeks burst into flame as his fingers stroke up my legs, but I don't move. I hold my delicate perch above him as his big hands curve over the tops of my thighs. His thumbs graze the sensitive skin where my legs meet my sex, and his fingers press into my ass as he urges me to shift forward.

The first slide of his tongue against the swollen lips of my sex is unexpected, which is ridiculous. His head is between my legs and he's pulling me toward his mouth. What did I think was going to happen?

But this is so much better than I ever could have hoped.

He's giving head like he kisses. With disorienting thoroughness. Long, slow tasting licks and sweet, hungry pulls.

He's giving head like a committed pervert. He's everything I wished for and more, and all of me throbs at the pleasure of his tongue between my legs. My breasts are heavy, my nipples tight, and deep inside me, arousal starts to pool.

I could come like this. Out in the open, riding his face.

My hands dip and sway as he urges my hips to rock against his mouth. Oh, yes. *I will come come like this*. He latches on to my clit and sucks, and the eagerness is enough to put me over the edge. It's a bright, sharp orgasm that shoots through me. I topple forward, but his hands shoot up and catch me, holding my body with superhuman strength as he licks me through the rippling aftereffects.

My head is spinning now. This isn't real. This is some kind of lust-induced dream, the way he moves me around effortlessly. He sets me down on the grass, then twists around and tugs me beneath him as we kiss.

He tastes like me, and my breath catches hard in my throat.

He tastes like he *feasted* on my body.

I push against him, first with my hips, then with my hands. I can't decide what I want next. I want it all. But first I want him on his back, so I can crawl down his body and take him in my mouth and on my skin.

"Not here," he whispers, palming my ass beneath my skirt as I try to wriggle south.

Right. We're out in the open, and he's in uniform.

"Sorry," I say, breathing hard.

"Nothing to be sorry about." He laughs and hauls me up for another kiss. "Christ, that was perfect. Come on."

He leaps to his feet and gives me his hand. I stand, way less graceful—because I'm still shaking—and he scoops me into his arms.

"Marcus!"

"Yes?" He grins at me as he strides back toward the office.

The porch creaks under his heavy steps, but he manages to swing the door open with ease.

I guess I can't protest his ability to carry me around.

He locks the door behind us, and I immediately wiggle out of his arms.

"Here, though, yes?"

He groans as I push him back against the desk, sitting him where he sat me, because turnabout is fair play, and I drop to my knees. "Yes."

I make short work of his belt, his zipper, and then his erection bulges out at me from behind the now-tight black cotton of his boxer briefs. Oh, Ranger Boy is most definitely Ranger Man.

My mouth waters. I've never wanted to give a sloppy blowjob quite as much as I do at this moment. But I still take a minute to appreciate this moment—the way his abs have pulled taught. The dark line of hair that disappears under the elastic I've hooked my fingers over. The veins popping on either side, next to those cut lines of muscles...

I lean in and lick along one of those delicious looking trenches.

He tastes like warm, clean man.

Oh, this mountain air is *amazing*.

"Poppy..."

I smile as he groans my name, his voice dropping into a rough, guttural note that makes me wet all over again. I may not like a BJ to be expected on a date, but come on—there's nothing better than the heady feeling of controlling a man from my knees.

Epic. Power.

I trail my finger down the same groove I've just licked, but I keep going. I tug his boxers down, and with my other hand, I catch his cock as it bounces out. Hello, Park Ranger.

Heat pulses through me as I stroke him. He's nice and heavy in my hand, warm and solid to the touch.

My crush was not misguided.

The mountain man appeal has delivered in spades.

In my peripheral vision, I see him clench his hands into fists and push them into his hips. That's nice. Polite. Considerate.

But I wanted a pervert. I grab one of his hands and bring it to the back of my head as I lean in and take my first taste of his erection. I slide the tip of my tongue over the velvety hard crown, circling the thick head before finishing my slurp over the slit right at the top, where a small burst of something delicious gets me humming.

Let's be real. Not all guys taste good to me. That's no reflection of them, just chemistry. Or lack thereof.

Marcus tastes *yummy*. Like, let me swallow him all the way down because yes, I want more of that essence in my mouth right now.

And as soon as I suck him in, he tightens his hand around my ponytail and that's even better. He doesn't push on my head. He does one better, and holds me back. He makes me work for it a little, although that's really a sham. His thighs are shaking from the first swallow, and it doesn't take long to push him over the edge.

I swallow that, too.

It's a brief respite from reality, but it's a perfect one.

I press my face into his leg and smile.

"Ah, Poppy." He groans and laughs and urges me to stand after he tucks himself away. "I was so wary of you when you arrived yesterday," he says as he tugs me between his legs. "I guess deep down, I've been waiting for someone to track me down. But no joke, Poppy, I'm glad you drove halfway up a mountain to find me."

"Me, too." I fold into his embrace.

"It's going to get worse out there, though."

"Shhh, be a buzzkill later," I whisper, and he laughs.

"I was going to offer you a place to stay out here. Should you need it."

I blink up at him. He's serious. And I don't think this is sex-related, although I'd probably—foolishly—say yes just for regular access to his tongue.

I wrap my arms around his waist and press my face into his neck. Stark sadness intrudes and I shove it away. Not right now, reality. You can intrude in a minute.

"Here's hoping the world stays upright enough that we don't see each other until Thanksgiving," I finally say.

He nods against my head. "We'll do our damnedest to make sure of it."

We stand like that for a while. He's warm, and his chest is lovely and firm to lean against.

But I have a flight to catch. And he has work to get back to.

"Before you go..." He squeezes my hand and reaches across the desk. He picks up a National Park Service keychain and hands it to me. "A souvenir."

I turn it over in my hand. "Thank you...?"

He chuckles. "Take out your phone."

Like we're going to exchange phone numbers, but we already did that.

I look at him carefully and do as he says.

He covers my hand with his, and with a firm push of his

thumb, extends the metal neck on the keychain fob. "Search for Bluetooth devices."

There's one new device nearby. I synch to it, and an app pops up on my screen.

What the what...?

Marcus keeps going. "Now that keychain can't be paired with any other device. It can't be read remotely. And if you notch the fob out like that again, it will immediately disconnect from your phone and take all the data with it. To reconnect, you do the same thing again. It's slick and safe."

I stare at him, then down to the keychain, then back to him. "Who are you?"

I expect him to say something cocky, like *Marcus Dane, park ranger*. Instead he gives me a serious look, then leans in to kiss me. "I'm just a guy in the mountains," he whispers against my temple as I slide my gaze over his shoulder to the bowl of keychains on his desk. "Trying to do the right thing."

CHAPTER TEN

MARCUS

POPPY HAS a rental car to return, so there's no need for me to drive her to the airport. I want to anyway, and she laughs and kisses my face as she tells me she'll see me soon.

I have to kiss her goodbye on the top of my mountain, tug her ponytail and promise to stay in touch.

Barely twenty-four hours have passed, but everything has changed.

I stand beside the spot where she parked until I can't hear her engine, then I stomp into my office.

The first call I make is to Toby.

"Long time no speak," he jokes with the care-free glibness of a man who's happy.

I'm not happy. "We need to talk."

"Good that you called me, then." He clears his throat and murmurs something under his breath. "Sorry, I'm in Toronto with Cara."

"Fun." But I say it in a hard way that makes it crystal clear I don't care. I'll care later. Cara's nice, although the last time I saw her she was practically a kid. The math promises she hasn't been a kid for a while, which is good, and probably the only reason Toby is still alive. Which is beside the point. "I—we—have a problem. Not an immediate one, but a future one."

"What kind of problem?"

"A reporter showed up here yesterday. She'd dug into my background, done some hard thinking, and was pretty sure I was a rogue Twitter tweeter."

"That's a mouthful."

"Shut up."

"I'm just saying, say that three times fast. Rogue Twitter tweeter."

"It's not funny."

"It really is. Because you're *not* a rogue—"

"She knows that now."

"She? The reporter?"

"Yeah."

There's a long, questioning silence. "Wait. You're not mad at this reporter? And you told her the truth. Who are you and what have you done with my wary-as-fuck best friend?"

I don't answer that.

"She must be some kind of something if you broke all your rules for her."

I sigh. "Don't worry about that. She's not the problem."

"Clearly not."

"Her name is Poppy, before you say something else that's going to piss me off."

He makes a long thinking sound. "Okay. So I'm not sure

what the problem is, then. You met a cute reporter, totally had a personality change, and convinced her you were a harmless teddy bear. Or something."

Fuck, that's shockingly accurate. "That's not the point."

"I—Okay. Sure. What's the point?"

"I haven't done a good enough job of covering my tracks."

"You mean the tracks of anyone and everyone you try to help in a retroactive way? No, you can't erase all of their blunders. That's the reality of it, and we knew that when you had this crazy idea. Don't worry about it."

"You'll be implicated."

"I have plausible deniability, but beyond that, I don't really care if anyone knows my politics align with well-intentioned internet rebels. That would probably do wonders for my stock price. Which you will benefit from, need I remind you?"

"You don't need to remind me, no." I swear under my breath.

"Make contingency plans. Meanwhile, we now have eight million people signed up for FishMail. Lemons, lemonade." It's his new fully-encrypted free email service. Like Gmail on protective steroids.

While I'm hiding in the shadows, Toby is about to step onto the main stage in the battle for individual liberty and free speech.

Poppy has a FishMail email address. I'm sure she uses it to protect her sources.

But some of the ass-monkeys who would troll her have those accounts, too. It's a double-edged sword that makes me uneasy because she needs to take self-defense workshops. And there I go again, worrying about Poppy when I've got business interests to protect.

Priorities, Marcus.

Except I don't think for a second that my priorities are backwards right now. Not at all. There's something special about her. I knew that the second her ponytail swished into view.

"She wrote an article about coming out here. It's not about me. It's about..." I rub my thumb into the corner of my eye. "Fuck. It's about a lot of good things, and I feel like a heel, and she's just left. And I don't know what to do."

"About the story? About the situation? Or about the girl?"

"All of the above."

"Okay. Well, I'm biased, but I like a good 'go all in to get the girl' approach. And as for the rest...have some faith. It'll sort itself out. Maybe it's time you slide out of hiding. Just a little."

I grunt. I hate that answer.

And I think the worst part is that he might be right.

Over the next few days, I manage to bury that thought under a pile of work. The week after Poppy leaves is a false return to normal. It's the height of summer and we're swamped with visitors, which means a lot of site inspections and too many rescues.

Four days go by and she doesn't phone. I start to regret leaving it open-ended when she left—call me soon, I'd said.

I should pick up the phone myself, but something is holding me back.

Is it a whole pile of secrets you're still keeping from her? Yeah, that's part of it.

But there's some baser shit, too. Like she stomped into my life and with one flick of her perky ponytail she had me rocked with feelings I'd long-thought myself immune to. I've spent fifteen years closed off to anything other than casual, no-strings fun—and sporadic fun at that—because when I was in California, I knew I wasn't sticking around.

Deep down, I knew from the start I was leaving, which is why when I invested in Starfish Instrumentation, it was as a silent partner. I didn't want to be part of Toby's grand plan. I just wanted to ensure he had the means to make it happen. And that investment—our investment, because my cousin Astrid went in on it too, with part of her inheritance—has paid us back handsomely, many times over.

Speaking of which...

I distract myself from thoughts of perky ponytails by logging into my computer at home and pulling up the latest prospectus package for Dane Capital. Astrid's the only person who calls it that, though. Officially it's a numbered corporation, and the capital funds are managed by an environmentally-conscious firm who finds us projects to contribute venture capital and seed money to—always anonymously.

We're picky. We get this packet of investment ideas every quarter and we usually pick one, maybe two.

Astrid has already read through it. There are digital post-it notes all over the files. I skim through them first. If she doesn't like a proposal, there's a slim chance I'm going to either, so those don't need as close a review as the handful she does like.

My cousin is hard to please.

We have that in common.

My phone lights up as I'm about to start reading the last

proposal. Poppy's name is on the screen, and my mood shifts hard into hungry predator mode.

"Hello, stranger," I growl into the phone.

She laughs like I'm no threat to her at all, and she's got that right. After the way I've been practically panting over her—both while she was here, and in her absence—the truth is she holds all the power here. I don't mind that at all. "Sorry it's taken me so long to call. I've been run off my feet since I've been back. Long days, short nights, zero time in between."

"I've been busy, too."

"Saving the world?"

"One amateur hiker at a time."

There's a nervous beat before she speaks again. "Is this a good time to talk?"

"Yeah. I'm at home." I rock back in my chair. "About to make myself dinner. How about you?"

"I just got home." She yawns. No shit—it's two hours later there than here, and I'm already eating late because I lost track of time in the prospectus.

"Have you eaten?"

"No." Another yawn. "Can you somehow make food happen through the phone? Is that part of your secret superhero skillset?"

"Sadly not."

"Meh. I'll make coffee and have a protein bar."

"Late night ahead of you?"

She sighs. "I haven't filed another story since I got back. Lots of leads, lots of words, but nothing has quite pulled together. Gotta get something done."

"What you are working on?"

"Um..." Another nervous beat. Should it be awkward between us? *Maybe you don't know her that well after all.* "Actually, I'm doing background for another Department of the Interior story."

Ah. I rub my jaw. "Lots of the stories there, I guess."

"Marcus, I won't—"

"Do your job, Poppy. Always."

She makes a little sound, like a stubborn sigh, and changes the subject. "I'm also working on a piece I'm going to shop around about the high-end escorts on Twitter."

I laugh. "That's unexpected and different."

"Maybe you'd be able to help me with that." I can practically hear the smile in her voice.

"Yeah? What do you think I know about high-end escorts—on or off Twitter?"

"Come on." Now we're both laughing, and this is more like it. Spar, baby, spar. "Are we pretending that you aren't a man of some means?"

Some. Yeah. At some point, I need to share more with her about that, but not in the middle of a conversation about hookers. "Continue with your wild assumptions, Reporter Girl. But I want it on the record I've never hired an escort."

"I have no trouble believing that, Ranger Boy. But you know people. You're observant."

"Now you're just flattering me."

"Is it working?"

"Sure. Tell me about your angle. What's the headline?"

"That's the problem. I don't exactly have one. I mean...there are high-end escorts on Twitter. Technology has shifted an industry. It's an interesting factoid, but beyond that? Dunno."

"But you feel like there's a story there."

"Yeah. I've followed a bunch of them on Twitter—"

"What?"

"On a secret account. My research account, it's fine."

I fire up another browser window. "Want to bet I can find that before we end this phone call?"

"There you go again, making me think you're more than meets the eye."

I'm already running a couple of scripts, looking for generic Twitter "egg" accounts that followed Poppy's official account first. There are...more than I expected. "Have you ever had a stalker?"

"Why?"

"No reason. Tell me more about the escorts."

"Marcus!"

I chuckle. "I'm looking at your followers. You have fans."

"I've had a couple of tweets go low-level viral. I get a burst of followers each time I do that, but it's pretty low-key."

For the most part. I see enough Pepe the Frog pictures to worry that she also gets some negative attention, but that'll have to be looked into in more detail when we're not on the phone. "Okay."

She hesitates, but then goes back to her original focus. "So the real question for me is whether or not this shift to social media has had any other significant effects—has it opened sex work up to women who previously didn't have access to clients, because they didn't want to work with a service, for example? And those numbers aren't reported to government agencies, obviously."

"Are there escort services going out of business? Some of

those would have government data you could request. From definitely-not-personal experience, my understanding is that they like to report taxes like good citizens."

She gasps. "And that might be an angle, too—social media cuts out the middleman, but it also cuts out the tax man."

"I'm hardly a newspaper expert, but that sounds like a headline."

"I could kiss you."

"I'll take a solid rain check on that. How does Thanksgiving sound?"

"Like it's a long ways away."

Yeah. I know the feeling. "Maybe we'll have a good excuse to cross paths before then."

"If I can get a good series of in-depth Interior pieces going, maybe."

I shouldn't give her any leads on that, but...what the hell. "Find someone in Washington to ask about plans for next year's entrance fees."

There's a long stretch of silence. I wait for her to ask me if they're going up, but she doesn't.

Good. I'd have to pretend I don't know, and I don't want to have to lie to her.

"Thanks," she finally says. "I'll find a way for that to come up."

I smile. "Are you going to be just as busy over the next four days?"

"Should I make more of an effort to keep in touch?"

"Yes." Simple as that. "I know we just met, but ..." *I want you more than I should. I want you more than makes sense.*

And simply, *I want you.*

"Yeah." Her voice catches. "I know."

"Are you going to make that coffee now?"

"I should."

"Can I call you tomorrow?"

"Please." A whisper. A promise she feels somewhat the same.

"Good luck with your stories."

When we hang up, I feel disconnected on more than just the literal level. I've tasted this woman. Held her in my arms. Fought with her and fought for her.

It was great to hear her voice. And it wasn't nearly enough.

We talk again the next night, and two nights after that. I text her a picture of the treed area just outside my office, and she sends back a cute-and-sexy selfie of her biting her lower lip.

We have phone sex the next night.

I make it a priority in my head to find a long weekend I can take off, but it may not be until September. Six weeks has never felt so long.

When Toby video calls on the weekend to run some ideas past me, he doesn't waste time after we conclude our business chatter. He rocks back in his chair and gives me an amused look. "You sound less grumpy than the last time we talked. Anything to do with Poppy the Reporter?"

"Maybe. We've talked a few times this week." For hours. "I like her. She's smart."

"That's a good sign. When was the last time you liked another human being?"

"I like all sorts of people."

He laughs.

"It feels like the real deal, though, crazy as that idea sounds," I confess. "I want to make her a mixed tape."

"Yeah, that's not a thing anymore."

"I know, I know. But like...a mixed CD. USB stick?"

He shakes his head. "Pretty sure kids these days just instant message each other a link to a Spotify playlist."

"That takes zero effort."

"Make a custom album cover for it."

"You've ruined this idea."

"Don't blame me. And don't blame the millennials, either, they're the future."

Stubborn optimist. "I regret telling you about Poppy."

"So it's not exactly casual?"

"I don't know." We got to third-base on a mountain top a few hours before she flew back to the east coast. And I haven't seen her since, but the sound of her shy little orgasm is still ringing in my ear. "It's complicated."

"What's the problem?"

"Distance."

"Jesus, man, there's an easy solution for that."

"I don't want to pressure her."

"I've married the world's least commitment-friendly woman, and even she liked the surprise appearance. Even if it's just for a night or two of hooking up...everyone likes orgasms."

"It's not just hooking up." I frown. I'm ninety-nine percent sure we're on the same page there. "And I don't want to talk about orgasms with you."

"Oh, you're *serious* serious." He sits up straight, him and his chair both snapping to attention.

"I didn't say that." I let a half-grin escape at the corner of my mouth. "But yeah, maybe. I mean, I want to fly across the country to see her."

"Do it. I did."

"And you got married. That might be a little too fast for Poppy."

He grins at me. "But not you?"

No, I don't want to marry Poppy.

Not yet.

But the idea is not completely horrible. It's actually very, very tempting.

Yeah, I need to get on an airplane and round that last base with my favorite reporter before Toby's inappropriate strategies take hold and I do something stupid like buy a ring for a woman I've only known for a week and only spent a few hours with at that.

"I'll fly out to see her soon, and that'll solve that problem."

"What are you waiting for?"

"Some of us have actual jobs, you know."

"I have a job."

"That can follow you on a plane."

"Surely you get time off. Wasn't that the whole point of joining the park service?"

"Not exactly. And it's complicated."

"You make it more complicated than it needs to be." Toby

cuts straight to the point, as he always does. And normally I'd blow him off, because I live the way I do for a reason.

But maybe my priorities can shift a bit.

"You have the means to go to her," he asks. "Why aren't you?"

Yeah. That's a good fucking question.

CHAPTER ELEVEN

POPPY

"THIS PIECE on the National Parks rate increases is excellent," the editor at The Washington Record says into my ear. I'm standing outside the Department of the Interior's giant concrete building in D.C., waiting to finish up this call so I can get in line at the hot dog stand.

"Thank you. I just got another quote from a local staffer at Interior, so that's three separate sources."

"Can we say senior staff confirm?"

"Mmm." I chew on my thumb. "Not really. Administrative level, lots of eyes on papers, if that helps."

"High-level access?"

"Yes, that works."

"Put that quote in and fire the final version over to me. We'll run it tomorrow. If it clicks, you can do another two in the same series. I want more the unintended consequences angle, that's unique." I do a fist pump in the air. "Plus people love park rangers."

I roll my eyes, but he's not wrong. The higher-concept a story, the more eyeballs we get on it. That's just how the world works. Plus...more stories... Screw it, I'm going to ask for what I really want. "I might need to conduct more research. Get back out there on the ground."

"Angling for another trip to Colorado?"

"Just a flight. Split the difference." I'll have a place to stay, I'm quite certain of it.

"Sounds good. Get on the next flight. After you file your story, of course."

My heart slams into my rib cage. "Of course."

He gives me a top three list of story ideas he could maybe get closer to the front of the paper, then I end the call and go and get myself a well-deserved hot dog.

I eat it on the way to a coffee shop, where I finish the article and fire it off. Then I dig into my emails. As part of my commitment to listening more than writing, I'm putting daily questions out there on Twitter. Asking people to DM or email me their stories, and I share them on their behalf, protecting their identities. Less reporting through a filter, more like a...narrative conduit.

Or something. I don't want to make it a bigger deal than it is. But it feels good. Today's question struck a nerve. I shared my own reality of having to work two and a half jobs, and asked people to share their own stories of struggling to make ends meet.

The answers are raw. College lecturers who need to use food stamps. A single mother who takes her son with her to nanny other children overnight because it's the most hours she can get. But through most of the answers, there's an unexpected thread—one of pride, like, this is insanity but they do it anyway and survive. Today feels like I'm finally figuring out what questions to ask. That they don't always fit with how I understand the world to be is disconcerting, though.

I grab ten more answers and schedule them to tweet out over the next hour, then I hop over to Expedia and search for flights to Denver. Another hit to the credit card, but I find a sale, and pray for the expense form to be approved sooner than later.

The cheapest flight is the last one that night. I call Marcus, but his phone goes straight to voice mail, so I throw stuff in a bag and decide to surprise him instead.

On the flight, I get an idea for a question of the day—how far people have traveled from where they live, and where they were born. It needs some polish, though. I don't want to weight it with my own bias. I'm still chewing on that when I land.

Marcus is still out of cell range, so I grab a free shuttle to the cheapest hotel around the airport.

I ask the driver about the furthest he's traveled from where he lives. He says probably Florida, for a family trip to Orlando. I ask him if I can tweet his answer, and he laughs. "Sure, lady. Whatever floats your boat."

Maybe that's not the best question of the day.

Dig deeper, I remind myself. It's easy to write the simple stories. But they don't grab readers by the guts and shake them hard. That's what I want to do.

Easier said than done, like almost everything worth doing.

I check in and fire Marcus a text to call me.

He does ten minutes later, and it's ridiculous how happy I

am to see his name on my screen. “Hi,” I say, pressing a hand to my belly to make the butterflies stop rioting. “Do you have any plans for breakfast in the morning?”

“Uh...” He clears his throat. “I was going to ask you the same thing.”

“You were?” I slowly push off the worn floral duvet on the double bed, the butterflies all flopping hard. “Where are you?”

“Dulles Airport.” He groans. “Why, where are you?”

“The Motel 6 on I-70.”

“You’re in Denver.”

“Yes?” I laugh because it’s ridiculous. “Oh, shit, Marcus! How long are you in Washington?”

“I’ll be back by the morning. This breakfast date is happening. Hang tight. *Do not move.* I’m coming to get you.” He growls something under his breath that sounds like *one more night.* I know the feeling.

I laugh weakly. “So much for a surprise, huh?”

“Yeah. Well...” He grunts, and I picture him shoving a hand through his hair. “How long are you out there?”

“A week, maybe. I can write from anywhere.”

“I have to work day after tomorrow, so that’s good. This is good.” He groans again.

“I’m sorry. You only had two days off and you flew across the country to see me?” Now I feel like shit.

“No, it’s fine. Really. Don’t worry about it.”

“Well, I do worry about it. Price of being my friend, is having me worry about you.”

“Friend?” He sounds amused. Like this is no big deal, but we’ve both flown in opposite directions because of a failure to communicate. This is a big deal. Why is he laughing? "Thank you for your friendly concern."

"You sound like..." I trail off. Fine if he wants to be a man of mystery, that's *fine*.

"Hey," he says softly. Marcus in a nutshell. He's so big, so strong, and yet gentle, too. My mountain man, literally. But still there are other layers I have no idea about.

Okay, maybe it's not fine.

"I'm not asking as a journalist," I whisper as I flop onto my side. "But why is this funny?"

"It just is. It'll be easier to explain in the morning."

"Do you remember what I asked before I left here?" *Who are you?* He'd given me a vague answer then, and suddenly I wonder if I'm being played for a fool somehow.

He sighs. "Why does it matter who I am?"

"It doesn't." It really doesn't *matter*, but it is relevant. How do I explain the difference? "But if I'm flying back and forth across the country to hook-up with someone—something that is a considerable expense for me, but totally worth it—I kind of want to know who he is."

"Oh, shit, Poppy. Of course, that's fair. And I don't want you to spend money to come see me. We can sort something out about that." He sighs. "I want you to know me. I do. Tomorrow, okay? I'll show you everything you need to know about me in the morning. Text me your room number. I need to grab some sleep before I head back."

"Okay..." I look at the clock. Jesus, he's going to try to catch the first flight out in the morning, which I think is at five. "Don't worry if you don't get a ticket. I've got work to do."

His laugh is muted. "I'm not worried. I just want to see you."

And the butterflies are back. Apparently they're immune to doubt. "Yep. Me too."

"Sleep tight?"

Hardly.

This is like sex Christmas Eve.

And just like while waiting for Santa, I do manage to drift off, then jolt awake at five, my heart pounding.

I drag myself into the shower. The steam feels good, and when I get out to a text message from Marcus, I feel even better.

Marcus: There in twenty. Wake up, sleepyhead.

That was ten minutes ago. I quickly dry my hair and put condoms in an obvious place beside the bed before firing back a response.

Poppy: I'm wide awake. And naked.

The knock at the door comes thirty seconds later. I jump at the surprise, then panic. I can't actually answer the door naked. I grab my sleeping t-shirt and pull it on, then run to the door. A quick glance through the peephole has my heart hammering a mile a minute because Marcus is on the other side.

And he looks *good.* Even through the fisheye distortion.

I pull the door open and he laughs as he steps inside, big and broad and mouthwateringly good looking. His gaze flicks down to my shirt, then back to my face, hot and laser-focused. "You're not naked."

"Had a little freakout about answering the door in absolutely nothing," I whisper as we come together, his lips brushing my forehead as I breathe in the scent of his skin. His hands smooth down my back. "But I'm naked under this shirt."

He pauses for a beat, his hands tightening on my waist, then he groans as he palms my bare ass.

I gasp as he hauls me up against him, then his mouth is on mine and my legs are around his waist. He growls words that make me ache for more. *Need. Crazy. Beautiful. Soft. Good. Taste.*

Somehow we get to the bed. It's only when I try to rip his shirt off him that I realize it's a nice button-down. And he's wearing dress pants, too.

"You dressed up? You look really good," I say. "Take off your clothes."

He grins. "You're the boss."

"We have unfinished business," I pant, stretching beneath him.

"I know." He tugs on the hem of my shirt, his knuckles grazing the crease between my leg and my pelvis.

I shiver, and his gaze turns molten.

"Hi," he whispers, his voice suddenly husky.

I give him a faint, desperate smile. "Hi."

His hand hasn't moved. His fingers are just inches from my bare pussy, and we're frozen in a locked-gaze tableau.

"I missed you." He lowers his head to kiss me again, and I part my lips, my eyes drifting shut as his tongue slides against mine. "So much," he adds against my mouth as he eases back. "And I want to take you so hard right now."

"Yes."

"Yeah?"

"Please, Marcus."

He crushes his mouth to mine again, and twists his hand at the same time, nudging my thighs wide. His touch is deft, erotic, and just hurried enough to reassure me that I'm not the only needy one here. He finds a way to ask me, in words or actions, if I want each step. His fingers inside me, his mouth next. Territory we're both happy to revisit. But he stops me when I try to roll him onto his back and telegraph my intent to taste him.

"Later," he growls. "I want inside you."

I grab a condom and slap it into his hand. He rises above me, rolls it on with quick, efficient movements, then he tumbles on top of me again. The next moment is a heady, throbbing pause as our bodies fit together. My legs curl up and spread for him. All of his muscles flex and shake as he levers his torso up, his hips down. The room is silent, our breaths loud, and the whole time, his attention is locked on my face.

Watching me, wanting me. I get lost in the heat in his eyes, and the rest dissolves away.

The thick press of his erection notches into place. He grins down at me as he drags his hand back up my body, his knuckles skating over my belly, around my breast, and up onto my neck. "So good," he murmurs, his eyes turning liquid. "You feel amazing already."

The first stretch takes my breath away. The second makes

me groan. He's perfect. Perfectly big, perfectly thick. Just the right size to make my brain go swirly and my pussy clench tight.

And the sound he makes as he bottoms out? Oh, sweet mother of mayhem, I'm going to remember *that* forever. Deep, guttural, needy... Yes. This was worth the flight to Denver.

A hundred times over. I wrap my arms around him as we begin to move. He plants his arms on either side of my head, caging me in.

I wrap my hands around his thick biceps. I love the feel of his skin, the solid flex of his muscles. I *love* the way he smells, the heat rising between our bodies, and the heavy weight of him on top of me.

We kiss again, and need ratchets inside me. More, yes, that, please.

Each thrust of his hips lights me up inside. Each adoring pass of his hand—on my breasts, my neck, his fingers on my lips—draws me higher and tighter, until I'm flying with how good it feels. Yesterday I was in Washington, chasing a story. Now I'm in Marcus's arms again. Lucky doesn't begin to describe how I feel.

"I want to see you," he says roughly. "Do you like being on top?"

"I like everything." I'm breathless and high as a kite, and as he slides out of me, a mad hunger takes over. I scramble after him, climbing on the second he rolls over.

I want to ride this man forever. I want to fuck him until I ache, until I know I'll feel him for the rest of the week, and then I want to fuck him just a little bit more to make sure.

He's just so...

Perfect. I smile as I roll my hips, as I raise up and lower down again, seating him deeper inside me.

"That good?" He looks up at me from beneath hooded eyelids.

"The best," I whisper. "You're so big."

He licks his lips and runs a lazy hand up my thigh. "You're tight and warm and I just—" He thrusts his hips up, making me gasp. "You make me big. You do this to me. All yours."

His words send a powerful thrill skittering under my skin.

He's all mine? Excellent.

I lean forward and brace myself against shaking headboard. "Are you mine to do whatever I want?"

"Anything," he growls.

I trail my fingers over his cheeks, across his lower lip. His tongue slides out and snakes around my fingertips.

I shudder as I drag those wet fingers down his body, slowly, carefully, until I touch us both where we're joined. I'll have to figure out some crazy things to do to him later, because right now, I just want to come.

"Fuck me," I whisper.

His gaze darkens and he settles his hands on my hips, holding me tight as he moves beneath me. My breasts sway and bounce, my clit rocks against my glancing fingertips, and deep inside, he swells even harder than before.

I close my eyes and tip my head back. God, yes. "Marcus." I breathe his name, over and over again, until I'm crying out at the same time as my body climaxes.

He shouts his own release, jacking his hips in a final, brutal thrust which he holds deep inside me for a long, throbbing beat before collapsing back against the bed.

I tumble to the side, still shaking from the after-effects of my own orgasm.

"Good morning," he finally says, his voice rich with laughter.

"Yeah. Nice to see you again." I bite my lip and twist to find his gaze on me, warm and inviting.

He looks around, his gaze lingering on the shadowed corners and the faded wallpaper. He gives me a lazy wink. "Nice hotel room, by the way."

I giggle. "Do you have someplace nicer we could be?"

"As a matter of fact, I do."

When we leave the motel, I don't see Marcus's truck anywhere, and ten seconds later a black sedan pulls up.

He gives me an inscrutable look, so I don't bother to parse what it means—but even if I had, I wouldn't have expected it to deliver us to an airport—and not the one I arrived at last night, either. We've gone across the city to a regional airport.

I press my lips together because the Uber driver doesn't need to know I have a million questions.

And Marcus is already fully aware. Out of the corner of the my eye, I see his mouth twitching. He's enjoying this. Well, that makes one of us. I don't even know what this is.

Marcus thanks the driver, shoulders my bag, and offers me his hand. "Coming?"

"Well, obviously," I murmur. "This could be a great story."

He laughs. "For our grandkids or a newspaper editor?"

"Why would you make me choose? Both sound like excellent options. I mean, depending on how this plays out."

He stops in the middle of the quiet terminal and kisses me softly, his hand squeezing mine between us. "I'm picking you up at the airport and taking you to my place. Nothing headline worthy here."

"Mmm." I glance around. "I was expecting more of the, uh, pick-up truck variety of ride. Not James Bond helicopter, or whatever you have planned."

He laughs. "No helicopter. And next time, I want you to tell me you can come out here, so I can fly you."

I push at his chest. "No! I'm not having you buy me plane tickets so we can have sex. Even if it is awesome sex."

He doesn't move. "Really awesome. But I wasn't talking about a plane ticket. I mean, *I* can fly you."

"Oh. *Oh*. You mean...literally...you can fly me..." My eyes go wide. I can't help it. That is not a normal offer. "I'm good with Delta. Me and economy class, we're like..." I twist my fingers together. "Plus all the points, you know. I like those."

"Sure." He grins. "Are you freaking out?"

"Yeah. You own a jet."

"A small one."

"You just fly yourself around wherever, like other people take a car."

"Something like that."

"So last night, when you called me..."

"I'd flown to Washington. I had a nap, and I flew back."

"I thought you made excellent time. But then you distracted me with your penis and I forgot to ask about that."

"My penis?" He's laughing at me again. Should I have said

cock? Delightful erection? The vocabulary rules for dating way outside one's socio-economic status is not clear. *He owns a jet.*

Marcus is in fact the guy I thought I might uncover for a juicy story. And then I went and fell madly in lust with him instead. "Can we not have this conversation in the middle of an airport?"

His grin gets wider. "Sure. Let's go have it on the plane. Do you want to sit in the co-pilot's seat?"

My laugh only has the tiniest edge of hysteria to it, and I'm quite proud of myself. "Sure. That sounds super normal."

We stop at a desk where Marcus signs off on a flight plan, then we head outside.

There's a little plane right in front of us.

It's...cute.

And small.

And we're totally getting on it.

Marcus has a plane.

I'm freaking out.

This is *great.*

But as soon as he shows me inside, my freakout fades. It's not a big plane. It has four seats in the main cabin, two right behind the cockpit, and that's really small.

On the other hand, the whole thing is *fancy*. Sleek white and black detailing, lots of leather with red stitching. This plane wasn't cheap.

He said he'd show me who he was.

Yeah, but I thought that meant going to his cabin in the woods and talking about our feelings. Maybe dig into why we don't like our parents as much as we should.

"Do you like your parents?" I blurt out.

He looks up from where he's checking some very complicated dials and switches in the cockpit. "In small doses."

I let out a sigh of relief. "Great. That's something we have in common."

"We have lots in common."

"Do we?"

He gestures for me to squeeze into the other seat in the cockpit. "Sure."

"We don't know each other."

"Then we have forty minutes to fix that before we land and I kidnap you."

"Cabin in the woods?"

He laughs. "Not a lot of trees around my place. But it's got a cabin feel."

I have to admit, skipping the four-hour drive from Denver to Rifle is lovely. And Marcus at the controls of a plane is an impressive sight. Plus we actually do get to talk about things we have in common.

Which is apparently coffee, sex, and disappointed parents, although the scale is a different.

"They liked the idea of me being a tech leader and being on the pages of Fortune Magazine," he says quietly.

"Ah."

"How about you? Why'd you ask about parents?"

"I, uh... haven't had any babies yet." My cheeks flame hot. Why did I bring up that line of conversation anyway? Ridiculous. "My brothers are younger than me, and all my cousins have kids, and... it doesn't matter. Thanksgiving will be swell, let's just say that much."

"You could skip it and come with me to Jake's wedding." The radio crackles to life, air traffic control advising him he can begin his descent, and the conversation is put on hold, which is for the best, because I don't know what my answer will be.

When we land, he introduces me to a scruffy kid named Jeff who is apparently going to park Marcus's jet for him, but the rest of their conversation is totally normal. Then we head to the dusty parking lot, where his truck is waiting for us. Actually normal.

We stop at the bakery, then the grocery store, more normal, then head out of town, climbing into the hills around the valley.

I'm not surprised when we drive down a long, winding lane and find what is definitely not a cabin in the woods. "Nice," I say when I find my voice.

It's a modern bungalow, crawling along a ridge. Low-profile, very high-tech. Definitely contributes to the super-spy alter-ego theory I have going.

The garage door opens automatically. He parks, then we walk back out to the driveway and up the front walk.

He stops me in front of the main door and turns me around.

The view is spectacular, the valley spilling out below us, the mountains glowing pink and orange in the distance on the other side.

"I'm a full-time park ranger," he murmurs in my ear. "And very private, for obvious reasons. This is hard to explain. But I told you I'd show you who I am. I was a seed money investor in Starfish Instrumentation. That proved lucrative."

I turn around, genuinely confused. "Why is that a secret?"

He rolls his neck and gives me a rueful smile. "Well..." He reaches past me and touches his hand to a sensor, unlocking the door. "Come on in."

"If this is where you tell me you're a spy, I've already figured that out."

He laughs out loud at that. "Not a spy." He sets my bag down inside the front door and gives me a chance to look around.

It does have a cabin feel inside, I guess. A reclaimed wood table dominates the space in the main room, with an open kitchen at one end and an oversized, well-worn sofa overlooking the valley at the other.

But I think there's a lot more house that crawls off in either direction, and Marcus is looking at me like he's trying to figure out how to say more.

Of course there's more.

"You don't need to—" I cut myself off and start again, because he wants to share, and I don't want to stop him. "How many people know you've invested well?"

"Not many."

I close the gap between us and wrap my arms around his tense body. "Thank you for trusting me."

"I didn't expect you to rocket into my life," he says gruffly. "I'm not transitioning well."

"By the standards of dating people in D.C., you're doing just fine. Once I went on five dates with a congressional aide before I found out he was married."

That gets me a serious growl.

"I didn't sleep with him."

"Good."

I laugh. "Anyway, I'm sorry I freaked out that you own a plane. You live in the middle of a big state, far from your friends, and you have the means, so that makes sense."

He leads me to the couch, where he flops out and tugs me down on top of him.

I nestle my head into the curve of his neck.

"I like flying," he says. "I thought about qualifying on bigger planes so I could work as a pilot. I still might. That's my backup plan if the park service gets too political."

"You wouldn't go back to investing?"

He clears his throat. "I never really left it. That's, uh, another thing. On a very part-time basis, I'm also something of a venture capitalist. I have a cousin who shares my love of the environment and together we run a non-profit that invests in big ideas."

Huh. "Cool."

We lie there for a few minutes, his hand trailing lazily up and down my back. The whole time, my brain is spinning, and finally I crane my neck up and give him a curious look.

"What?"

"What kind of big ideas, exactly?"

"I just gave this guy I know some money to invest in wind-powered shipping."

My lips repeat those words. *Wind-powered shipping.* "Like five hundred years ago?"

"It wasn't that long ago that we stopped using sails, but yeah. Like that. It's a renewable resource, and with a combination of carbon-fiber sails and smarter engines, we can cut the energy consumption of massive ships by up to ninety percent."

"And this guy you know? Shipping?" I spin through the

rolodex in my head. I scramble off him and start to pace. "Is that Ben Russo?"

He stands, too. "You already know we're friends."

"Right. But that was like, college drinking buddies. Not... You invested in Toby Hunt's company as a start-up. Now you're a major investor in the future of Gladiator Industries."

"Minor partner in one project."

"Stop correcting me. This isn't on the record and I don't really care about the details."

"You asked."

"I was not prepared for the answer. So you're like..." I try to do the math and give up. Marcus is definitely a billionaire. That's a whole new level of we have nothing in common. "Okay. Does this place have a big-ass bathtub? I want a bubble bath."

"It has three. You can take your pick—on one condition."

"What's that?"

He grins wickedly. "I'm joining you. You can feel free to grill me some more."

CHAPTER TWELVE

MARCUS

POPPY in a bubble bath is exactly as hot as I imagined, which shouldn't be where my head is at right now, but I can't help it.

She's slick and soapy and flushed. I want inside her.

Instead, I'm letting her decorate me with bubbles while she figures out what she wants to ask me next.

It's a sweet torture.

I don't exactly fit in the tub, even though it's officially big enough for two, so my arms are up on the sides and my legs are bent.

Poppy's kneeling in front of me, sloshing water gently. Wet strands of her hair trail over her shoulders and around her breasts. "I just want to be sure that you aren't pulling a fast one on me," she says. One corner of her mouth quirks up as she gives me a gentle look. "And I guess by admitting that, I'm saying I trust that you aren't."

I reach out and trace one of the dark lines where the end of her hair curls over her sweet, pale flesh. "But you think you shouldn't trust me. I agree, by the way. You shouldn't trust anyone."

"I do, though. There's something about you. It's a special kind of madness, how I feel about you. Like I look at you and..."

"And you really see me?" I follow the strand of hair up to her collarbone and onto her neck, where her pulse flutters under my touch. "I feel the same way. I see you, Poppy. And I like you. More than I should. More than is safe. Not because I can't trust you. I can, and I do. But because you make me want things..."

She grins at me as I trail off. "Is question time over?"

"Not at all," I say huskily. "Ignore the erection bobbing in the water in front of you. Nothing to see here."

She takes me in hand, and I groan from how good it feels. "Feels like something."

"Maybe question time is over after all."

"Paused."

"Sure." I haul her on top of me. I wasn't talking about sex, exactly. She makes me want a whole lot more than fucking, but this is a good start.

I purposefully left the condoms on the other side of the room so we could talk, so instead of sliding into her, I rock my erection between her folds, sliding her slickness up and down the underside of my shaft. We kiss, hot and hard, and it doesn't take long for her to quiver and shake in my arms.

I hold her through the first orgasm, then roar out of the water, holding her tight. I grab a towel and wrap it around her, spinning her around to look in the mirror over the wide wall-to-wall vanity.

Where the condoms are.

"Bend over," I tell her, holding her gaze in the mirror.

She bites her lower lip and does as she's told, letting the towel fall against the marble first as a cushion. I gather her wet hair, twisting it gently to the side, baring her spine.

Starting at the nape of her neck, I taste her skin, following the vertebrae down her back in a lazy, teasing slide of my tongue. She sighs, a long, groaning exhale, and rocks her hips back against me. I settle my hands there, squeezing her tight as I reach the curve of my bottom.

"Spread your legs."

Again, she does as she's told, and my cock throbs.

I find her slick, arousal coating her plump pussy, and when I stroke around her clit, she jolts against me.

Good.

Condom on, I line up behind her and surge forward, sinking fully into her tight heat on the first thrust. Fuck, she feels amazing.

I look at the mirror again, where she's watching me, eyelids low and mouth all flushed.

That mouth. Fuck me.

I pick up the pace. "Touch yourself."

"Bossy today," she says, and I grin.

"Do it."

She does it. And when she does, her cunt flutters around my cock.

"Get yourself off," I growl. "Make yourself come. Make me feel it." I slap her ass lightly, then sink my fingers into her pink flesh.

She slaps her free hand against the mirror, urging me on. We stare at each other's reflections as she rubs her sweet little pussy and I drive my cock into her depths over and over again. When her body tenses up, as she pushes back against me, I lose control and rut against her like a madman. Deep inside, she spasms hard. Her orgasms pulls my own release, urging me to spill my come deep inside her body. I imagine the condom's gone, and growl her name with the first spurt.

God. Fucking. Damn.

Even as my cock is still jerking inside her, I wrap my arms around her body and bury my face in her wet hair. Poppy, Poppy, Poppy.

The things I want with this woman are damn scary. Forever kinds of things.

Slowly, we disentangle. I get rid of the condom and grab more towels. I gently sit her on the counter and dry her hair as she brushes my face with sweet butterfly kisses.

"What time do you need to go to work tomorrow?" she asks lazily.

"Seven."

"Kay."

I smile and kiss her forehead. "You can sleep in."

"I need to do some work, so I'll get up with you." She gives me a brilliant smile. "And we still have the rest of today."

"We do."

"What do you want to do?"

Find out more about how you feel about babies. "Go for a walk. Show you the rest of my world."

She lets out a happy sigh, and I realize it doesn't fucking matter how she feels about babies. "That sounds amazing."

"And I should feed you some lunch, too."

She laughs. "And now you're officially perfect."

CHAPTER THIRTEEN

POPPY

I SPEND the next week at Marcus's house, getting used to dating a billionaire who gets up while it's dark and goes to work as a park ranger because he likes that better.

I'm starting to get that he's not so much an enigma as a true exception. Sure, he keeps things close to his chest, but he is exactly what he says he is—quiet, steady, and very into me.

Some days he drops me in town when he goes to work, some days I stay here and wear nothing but one of his shirts while I write.

It's magical.

And early one morning it all comes to an unexpected end with an email from my editor at the Record.

We're still in bed when I read it.

"Oh," I say, sitting up.

"Is that a put-on-coffee kind of oh?" Marcus asks as he peers at the clock. It's five-thirty here, so not insanely early back in Washington.

I shake my head. "No. It's not breaking news or anything like that. It's...a job offer of sorts." I read the highlights of the email out loud to him. I've been tapped to be a new part of a team at the Washington Record tasked with compiling long-form narratives about significant events. "It sounds pretty cool. The LA Times has been doing something similar and we've talked about it, but it takes a lot of intensive research and time in the field. Huh."

He settles his hand on the back my neck and rubs gently. "That sounds great."

I'm sad about saying goodbye to Marcus again, of course, but it's the kind of writing I want to do. I chew on my lower lip. "And I'll be able to come back here more often if I'm not hunting for stories of my own on the streets of Washington," I tell him.

"You don't need to convince me," he rumbles. "It sounds like a good fit for you."

"I'm convincing myself."

"Ah." He slides his knuckles along my jaw, then lifts my chin so I'm looking at him. My heart melts when he smiles. "What do you want to do?"

I hold up my phone. "This."

"Excellent. When do you need to be back in Washington?"

"In three days."

His eyes go soft. "Perfect. We'll have time to celebrate properly."

He rolls me over and wakes me the rest of the way up with a slow, hard fuck into the mattress.

After, I sit on the bed and watch him move around his room naked, getting his uniform ready before we have a shower. He's all thick muscle and warm skin. Just enough hair to draw the eye to the good parts, and a ruthless indifference to being watched.

"Are you watching my ass again?"

Or maybe not. "It's my favorite part of your body."

He turns around, his semi-soft, always thick cock bobbing into view, and my mouth goes dry.

"One of them, I mean."

He laughs and I drag my gaze up to his face. I'm sure I'm blushing, and I don't care.

"Come here?" I don't care that it comes out like a plea. He can know how much I want him.

He tumbles on top of me, his weight heavy and welcome, and I steal the kiss I want. Deep, soft, lingering.

"How much of that can we cram into the next seventy-two hours?" I ask when he lets me up for air.

"As much as we need to last us until November."

"Your friend's wedding..."

"I was serious about you coming with me."

In my circles, a wedding plus-one invite is more about appearances than significant feelings, but Marcus isn't like that at all. He's serious about a lot more than our next date.

"This is insane, you and me," I whisper as I crawl on top of him. Our bodies are sweat-slicked and sated, but we fit together just right, and that fires something up inside me. Not just arousal. Something deeper.

A connection.

I don't care that I smell like sex, that we both need showers.

I like the smell of Marcus on my skin. And from the possessive way he's buried his face in my neck, I'm pretty sure the feeling is mutual.

"Come with me," he murmurs roughly. "Don't over think it."

"That's impossible. The overthinking, I mean. Going with you to a wedding sounds really nice."

"Nice?" He howls. "Death by faint praise." He rolls me onto my back and gives me an amused smile. "What can I do to elevate it to pleasant?"

I swallow hard. "Well, it's going to be Thanksgiving...and my family gets together in New Jersey..."

His eyes go wide, and for a second I think I've misread him. "Family?"

"Yeah." *Stand your ground, Lisowski.* "My parents live in Chicago, but my brothers both go to school on the east coast, so...we do Thanksgiving at my aunt and uncles in Hoboken. I mean it's going to be awful, of course. But maybe it could be awful for us both. Together."

He rolls onto his side beside me and rubs his hand over his perfectly scruffy jaw. My heart hammers in my chest as he thinks about it, his brow drawing tight for a painfully long stretch before he shrugs. "Well...that might be nice, too."

My pulse rockets as I push at his shoulder. "So mean."

"All's fair in love and war," he murmurs, pouncing on me again as we kiss.

War—that's been us from the start. Tension and sparring and...

Lust. Definitely that, too. An attraction unlike anything else I've experienced. Was that the start of love? A connection at first sight, one born out of kismet and chemistry instead of the slow-growth friendship I always expected to be the foundation for love?

That night, we go out for BBQ.

"Revisiting the scene of our first date," Marcus says, grinning at me.

"Really terrible date. You stormed out and I yelled at you."

"Yeah, but then you told me you had a crush on me, and all was right with the world. Now eat your ribs."

I gaze at him happily across the table. Despite the lovely house and the fancy plane, I still can't quite picture him with his friends. "Tell me about this wedding," I say, licking sauce off my thumb. "It's in New York?"

He nods. "At the Plaza. Fancy all the way."

"You'll be in a suit?"

He groans. "And a tie. I don't mind dressing up, but the tie always kills me."

"I bet you'll look hot as... you know."

He laughs out loud. "Say it, Poppy."

"Hot as..." I lower my voice. "Fuck."

He winks. "Definitely."

"You're terrible. Tell me about your friends."

"You know about them. You have dossiers on them."

"Not the official stuff. Tell me what I need to know to make a good impression on them. As your...date."

"As my girlfriend."

Now I'm grinning. "Okay. That too."

"Just be yourself?" He laughs deeply as I mock-glare at him.

"Okay, okay! Uh...we all met in Boston. I'm a couple years older than them. Jake and Toby were roommates the first year, in my building, although I didn't get to know them until the summer. I was a student residence assistant that summer, for the kids who stuck around for summer school. It didn't take long for me to realize they were a scary smart pair, and by the end of the summer, they had a plan to take over the world. I somehow got tangled up in that. Not that I minded at the time."

"When did you meet Ben?"

"Two years later? Jake sped through his degree as fast as he could, and he started at Harvard while Toby and I were still at MIT."

"What were you doing then?"

"Uh..." He gives me a lopsided grin. "A second Masters degree. I couldn't figure out what I wanted to do, basically. And I was spoiled. I had a small trust fund that allowed me to keep going to school as long as I was down with eating a lot of rice and beans."

"That's not most people's definition of spoiled," I murmur, searching his face.

His expression tightens. "Yeah. But it was still a gift many don't have."

I nod. "Right. So you were really a guy they looked up to."

"Or the guy who was willing to buy them beer. Maybe a bit of both."

"Bad RA."

"It was a short-lived career. The first of many."

"Maybe you're just a nomad. Nothing wrong with that."

He scratches his temple. "Yeah. It feels weird when you're surrounded by hyper-driven people, though. Like Jake—he's a natural businessman. That's what he's meant to do, you can just tell." Marcus's expression softens again. I really like how fond he is of his friends. "He can solve any problem faster than anyone I've ever known. He looks at things differently. Last year, he acquired SwiftEx, and everyone thought that was a terrible move, right?"

I'm not a biz reporter, but yeah, I remember that. And in the last six months, he's completely turned the business around. "Noted. Never underestimate his ability to see things."

"Do you know that's how he met his fiancé? Through SwiftEx? This is good to know before the wedding, although I'm sure they'll tell the story then, too."

"Did she work there?"

He shakes his head. "She was a customer. And he went undercover as a delivery driver—which is how he figured out how to turn the company around, by the way. Anyway, she thought he was a relief driver, and they kept talking every time he came to her door...one thing led to another, and here they are."

"That's one of those stories you tell the grandkids."

"For sure. And you'll love Jana. She's down-to-earth. I met her earlier this year when I was in New York for a weekend."

"And what about Toby and... what's his wife's name?"

"Cara."

I nod. "How did they meet?"

"Cara is a Russo. Ben's little sister. So they would have met when we went to the Hamptons the first summer with him, probably. Or maybe on a weekend trip into New York. Needless to say, Cara wasn't on Toby's radar until recently."

"And Ben's still single?"

Marcus nods. "Yeah. And a massive flirt, be warned."

"Duly noted."

He takes my hand across the table, and we both stop talking. His face goes serious, the lines that carve out his features deepening as he gives me a solemn look. "You're going to impress the hell out of them. They're going to wonder how I ever scored you."

"What will you tell them?" I try to smile, but fail. "That I hunted you down for a story?"

"They already know that." He takes a deep breath. "This new job. You're going to have a bigger profile. More people paying attention to you. Stay safe, okay?"

I nod. I'm not stupid.

We finish eating, then drive back to his place, a new heaviness hanging over both of our moods.

He brings up safety again once we're inside. "I was thinking—and tell me if this is overstepping—that maybe I could show you some self-defense stuff. I know you took workshops, but—"

"Yes." My pulse races.

"Yeah?"

"I'd love that." I jab at him playfully. "Plus, sparring with you could be hot."

He laughs. "Not the point I was going for, but..." He grapples with me until we end up kissing. "Okay, yes. Hot. But focus, too. I want you to be able to kick my ass for real. Which means you need to be ruthless and wicked."

I nod, my ponytail bobbing. Sure. Wicked. I can pretend to be that...

"Your sweet as apple pie appearance is actually an advantage," he says, reading my mind. "People will underestimate you. Let them."

I swallow hard. "Got it."

"Okay, so this is what we're going to do..."

He takes me downstairs to his gym—more rooms I hadn't yet explored in his secretly massive house—and walks me through some basic holds I'm already familiar with from the workshops I've done. Then he tries to get me to put them together into some real moves, which is tricker.

After he takes me down to the mat two times in a row, he takes my hands in his. "Let's try that again, and this time, get mad at me. For real. I'm every jerk who has made you feel threatened in any way, shape, or form. Remember, angry assholes expect you to go one way. Go the other. Move in, twist toward them, drop low. Show me that you're not afraid of me." He steps right into me, looming big, and he grabs my shoulders in his hands. I can feel how he's curved his fingers around my body, how he's digging into my shoulder blades so I can't run.

And when I tug back instinctively, he sneers at me and tightens his grip to the point of hurting.

I lunge forward, slamming my body against his, then I drop to the ground and roll away, kicking at his legs.

He doesn't topple over as I wanted him to, but he hops, and that's enough. I'm up and sprinting to the wall, which I touch just as he grabs me again.

This time when he puts his hands on me, he's gentle. I twist in his arms and climb up him. He presses me against the wall and kisses me, a desperate plea. *Don't get hurt.*

"I'll be safe," I promise him. "And we can try that again tomorrow. Every day until I leave."

"Take me down over and over again until you feel confident in it, okay?"

I squeeze him tight. "Promise."

He carries me into his room and we crawl under the blankets naked. He's gentle there, too, until he's not, and it's perfect both ways.

CHAPTER FOURTEEN

MARCUS

THE DAY BEFORE POPPY LEAVES, there's a staff party, and she comes with me.

"By the time we get to Jake's wedding, we'll be counting our dates well into the twenties at this rate," she teases as we arrive at the picnic area.

"I should be so lucky. Besides, you may be so busy between now and then that I might not see you. I need to cram in all the goodness now."

"I can get creative on the phone," she whispers before kissing me on the cheek and hopping out of my truck.

I know she can. I grin and follow her.

She holds my hand as I introduce to everyone. When I get to Brianne Fischer—my young staff member who is actually responsible for the rogue Twitter account Poppy suspected me of being behind—Poppy acts like this is the first time she's heard Brianne's name. Bri turns pink.

My girlfriend could teach her some lessons in playing things cool. If Brianne is ever outed for real, I'm going to have to hide her on the top of a mountain to protect her.

After making the rounds for introductions, we settle into camp chairs near the grill and Poppy gets a front-row seat for sharing time, when we all confess the weirdest things we saw from park visitors over the last week or so. There are the usual wild animal encounters, but after a few of those stories, one of the other junior rangers nudges Brianne.

"Tell them," he says. "About..." And he waggles his eyebrows.

I groan. There's no way this is a story any supervisor should hear.

Brianne looks at me, and I clear my throat. "Should I go and grab a beer while you tell the group?"

"Umm... Okay, well... I may have interrupted a threesome."

Sex in the park is kind of a regular thing, but more than two people is less common. "Oh?"

She gives more graphic details about a threesome she interrupted halfway up one of our most popular hiking trail, and the tall tale they tried to spin about having a permit for recreational activities. "I told them I was pretty sure under the same area of the park service regulations was a sub-regulation about taking their picture and posting it to Facebook."

I swear under my breath. "Please tell me you're kidding."

"So you're in a better than average mood, but your sense of humor is still stuck to bone-dry?" she asks innocently.

"There's nothing wrong with my sense of humor."

Beside me, Poppy is giggling uncontrollably.

I look at her.

"What?" She grins. "Clearly she was kidding." She looks at Brianne. "Right?"

"Sure." Brianne winks.

Poppy laughs harder, and I go to get that beer after all.

When I get back, Brianne is sitting in my chair, and everyone else has moved into the pavilion, setting up for dinner.

I stop beside Poppy's chair as she says, "If you ever want to talk, off the record, you know where to find me. I promise I don't want to out you."

Brianne looks over at me.

Poppy shakes her head. "Oh, I wanted to out *him*. He's a story. You're part of the process. My interest in you would be strictly limited to reaching people higher up the food chain than you."

"Hey," I protest.

"Past tense," she says, winking up at me.

"Don't past tense me. I know what that means."

"Stay nimble, Ranger Boy," she whispers as I lean in to kiss her. "You never know when I'm going to get you."

Oh, she's got me all right. She's got me good.

"She's not exactly I pictured," Poppy says as we're driving home.

"Who? Brianne?"

"Yep. She's sweet. And young. She's really a rogue tweeter?"

"She's tougher than she looks." I pick up Poppy's hand and kiss her knuckles. "A lot like you."

"I look tough," she protests.

I grin. "Of course."

"You thought you could eat me alive, and you didn't."

"I sort of did." A lazy, pleased smile spreads across my face and her cheeks pink up.

"That's filthy," she whispers.

We're both thinking of my tongue between her legs. I want to go down on her again right fucking now. Slow and deliberate and hungry.

"I'm filthy," I murmur instead. "Haven't you figured that out yet?"

"I know." The hitch in her voice is my undoing.

I step on the gas. "Ten minutes to my place, Poppy."

"Is that a promise or a threat?"

I throw my head back and laugh. This woman is everything. "Both."

But when we get home, I find myself wanting to confess something other than dirty thoughts.

She gets to the door first. I catch her around the waist and squeeze her tight as I kiss her neck. "So...just in case you were ever in the neighborhood..." I trail my fingers down her arm and circle them around her wrist. "I was thinking you might want to be able to get into my house even if I weren't here."

"In case I was in the neighborhood?" She twists her head to look at me with a smile on her face.

"Yeah."

"Okay." She laughs gently as I lift her arm and press it to the security scanner. "Like this?"

"Twenty-first-century version of giving you a key."

"Most people still just do the key thing."

"I'm not most people. Hold still."

I log in to my security system on my phone and add her as a user, then tell it to scan her hand to record the print.

"This is a complicated way to get my fingerprints," she whispers. "You could have taken them while I was sleeping."

"What makes you think I didn't?"

She laughs harder and her hand shifts.

"Hold. Still. Now I need to scan it again."

"When am I going to be here when you aren't?"

"Whenever you want."

She gives me another curious look. "Really?"

The system beeps, accepting her handprint, and the door unlocks. I gesture toward it. "After you."

"Well, that's really nice," she says as she opens the door. "And I didn't get you anything."

"You came to visit me for a week and a half. That was pretty awesome."

She wiggles her fingers. "And now I can come back whenever I want."

"Exactly." I prowl after her as she moves restlessly through the house. This is our last night together for a while, and it's put us both a little on edge.

She stops in my bedroom door, spinning around just as I catch her again.

The look we share is hot enough to incinerate all of Rifle, but I'm not ready to get naked and fuck her just yet. There's something else I want to say.

"From the first second I saw you, I wanted you," I tell her hoarsely. "I wanted you when you were digging into my life, I wanted you when you were yelling at me. That first day in the truck, when I thought you were seducing me for a story, I wanted to give in. You can have me however, whenever you want. I'm yours."

"That scares me a little, in a good way," she whispers. "I didn't see you coming. I don't know what to do with you."

"Yeah." I kiss her temple. "I know the feeling."

"I'm yours, too," she admits. "In every way. I know it's crazy to say that, but..."

"I'm falling in love with you." There. I said it.

She blinks at me.

I clear my throat. "Too soon?"

She bursts into tears. "No. God, I'm going to miss you so much."

I pull her into my arms. "Good?"

She nods into my chest and mumbles something I can't make out. I kiss the top of her head and she mumbles again.

"Baby, I can't hear you."

"I'm leaving my heart here with you," she says, lifting her face again. "Just so, you know, you can finish that whole falling in love thing while I'm gone."

I pick her up and she twists her arms around my neck as I kiss her. Her mouth tastes like lemonade and happiness, and I lose myself in her.

I may have her heart here, but she's taking mine with her, too.

God damn it. We should have seen this coming, but even if we did, I don't think either of us would want it any other way.

CHAPTER FIFTEEN

POPPY

November
Portland, Maine

I'M in Maine with three other members of the Record's reporting team for a contentious candidate debate leading up to a special election called to replace the junior senator for that state.

We aren't alone in being here. All the national media has descended, along with protestors, supporters for both candidates in the election, and a good number of general gawkers.

In addition to doing background for our story, I've been live tweeting all day. First outside the suburban arena where the debate is being held, and now inside.

There's definitely a hostile energy in the cavernous space. I tweet out pictures of the crowd as I move through it. There's a cordoned-off press area, and I wait until I get there before clipping my badge to my chest.

James and Guiliana are having a spirited discussion about how long the civil debate will last before it devolves into a shouting match. I take up a position on the outside of Guiliana and do what I've been doing a lot of lately. I listen. First to the reporters around me—more of the same argument, plus lots of grumping about the bullshit early timing we had to make in order to get our press credentials.

Then I step as far as I can get to the side and try to listen to the crowd, but it's hard, because the music is loud and the people around us aren't talking.

I'm tempted to head back into the throngs of people, but there's something about that negative energy gives me pause. Maybe today isn't the day to dive deep into what people are feeling.

Boundaries are healthy, Marcus would say.

He's going to be proud of me when I tell him I stuck to the press area. Bah. Being one of three dozen people back here isn't great reporting, though.

My Twitter mentions are getting busy, which makes it impossible to find responses I need to reply to. Crap. I tighten up that filter, then tweet another update that we're fifteen minutes out from the start of the debate.

When I look up from my phone after doing that, there's a guy standing right in front of me on the other side of roped off press pen.

He's holding a phone, too, and I'm pretty sure he's looking at the Twitter app.

I can't step back because there's a camera guy right behind me, so I move to the side.

Dude mirrors me. His expression twists in pure anger. "Lügenpresse," he sneers, and I force myself not to recoil. *Lying press*. Great, an actual neo-Nazi.

Despite their virulent presence on social media, these kinds of protesters aren't everywhere. And we didn't get any heads-up that we'd be expecting them today.

"How are you enjoying the debate?" I ask him, proud of myself for keeping my voice calm. I slide my hand into my pocket and flick the Bluetooth interceptor Marcus gave me ages ago. I've been using it a lot lately, and quietly distributed them to other reporters, too.

Apparently Toby is thrilled they're useful.

Right now, I'm grateful for the device, because Angry Dude slaps at the phone and swears at me, a string of words I can't publish in The Record and wouldn't be interesting enough anyway.

This asshole isn't a story, he's a distraction. But if he gets ahold of my phone, that's bad news.

I jerk my hand back, but not quick enough, and he's got me by the wrist all of a sudden. My phone tumbles out of my hand, landing on the concrete floor with a sharp smack.

Shit, shit, shit...

I try to look for it, but he's got a tight grip on my arm.

"Let go of me," I hiss through gritted teeth. "Get your hand off my body."

"Hey," someone yells, and I can feel the heat of the camera lights turn my way.

Aw, crap. I don't want to be the story. I hear Marcus's voice in my head. *Angry assholes expect you to go one way. Go the other. Move in, twist toward them, drop low.* I step forward, my mind spinning as I try to figure out where his fingers end, where the weak spot is.

This isn't anything like how we've practiced over the last few months. This is terrifying, and I'm shaking as I tentatively turn my hand.

The asshole's grip tightens.

Fuck, fuck, fuck.

He sneers as he jabs his other hand out, grabbing my hip. I can smell sweat on his skin, see the pores on his face, and the hard, sharp anger in his eyes.

He's pissed at me. He doesn't even know me, but it doesn't matter.

I represent all that's wrong in his world, and he's going to take it out on me. His grip tightens and I cry out despite myself. It really hurts. But as I buckle inward, I realize he's left his body wide open.

On pure adrenaline, I jerk my knee up, making contact with his groin. At his startled, wincing gasp, I jerk my hands together and drive them up his body, slamming the heels of my hands into the underside of his jaw.

He staggers back, and I do the same, slamming into one of my colleagues in the press.

"Sorry, sorry," I gasp, twisting around. Shit, James is on the ground.

He waves his hand. "I'm fine. Are you okay?"

I nod roughly as he hops back up. "Sure. My wrist hurts." I rub at the reddened skin there and wince as I hit a tender spot. I turn to glare at the neo-Nazi as he's being hauled off the ground by security.

"Poppy, what did he say to you?"

I turn around and am blinded by a camera's light. "He called me Lügenpresse," I say, finding my voice. "That was it. I asked him how he was enjoying the debate, and then he grabbed me. It's over."

"Will you press charges?"

Jesus Christ. We're vultures, even when it's one of our own. I give the guy asking the questions—a local CBS affiliate reporter, not someone from the national circuit—a faint smile. "I was assaulted while doing my job. Whether or not that was criminal is a question for the local police." I hold up my wrist and wriggle it. "I'm not injured. Just shaken up. I'm fine. Has anyone seen my phone?"

A security guard tries to stop me as I duck under the rope barrier.

"Excuse me, I'm looking for my phone."

"Ma'am, you'll need to stay where you are until the police get here."

"Why? Did I do anything wrong? I was just protecting myself and now I can't find—"

"Your phone. Yes, ma'am, I understand. However—"

I suck in a frustrated breath. Okay. Fine. This is why I use that Bluetooth device. "Gotcha. I'll just wait right here while people trample all over my phone."

He gives me a sympathetic look, and after I return to the press side of the barrier, he looks around, but my phone is gone.

The police arrive a few minutes later, and I'm taken to a room elsewhere in the arena to give a statement. They offer to take me to the hospital, but I really am fine.

We're almost done when there's a loud banging on the door.

I jump. Okay, maybe I'm not completely fine.

One of the officers opens the door, and as soon as I hear the concerned voice on the other side, I stand up. "That's my boyfriend," I say. "Let him in."

"We have a few more questions."

"He wasn't here before, and—" Marcus shoves the door open, and I shrug. "He's not going to take no for an answer, so..."

"Excuse me, sir, you'll need to wait outside."

Marcus shakes his head. "Yeah, that's not going to work for me. Why wasn't there a police presence near the press area? Why was there only a single rope barrier? You go and get your supervisor. Tell him I have some serious questions for him, and if he doesn't want to answer to me, he'll be answering to the governor within the hour."

Hello, pissed-off billionaire boyfriend.

I give him a wide-eyed look. *I'm fine,* I try to convey.

He ignores that and glares hard at the cop. "Go. Now."

The cop goes.

"That wasn't necessary," I whisper under my breath as Marcus hugs me.

"I'm glad I was on the east coast already." He kisses the top of my head. "I flew in this morning for a suit fitting in New York with the guys."

The wedding is next weekend, and Marcus has mentioned he has other business in New York, too. I was going to fly down in two days.

Something tells me he's going to want me to fly back with him tonight, and I'm not likely to argue. It's not like I can objectively report on today anyway.

"Have you had anything to eat or drink since it happened?"

"No. I'm not hungry."

"Good to have something anyway to combat the shock." He raises his voice. "You. Get her some juice. Cranberry if you can find it, it's her favorite."

"Stop bossing around the cops," I whisper. "And how did you know what happened?"

"It's all over the news." He hesitates. "But I was already on my way here. There was chatter I didn't like on the alt-right forums."

"About tonight?"

He doesn't answer.

"Marcus?"

"About you."

"Seriously?" That makes me *mad*. "Why?"

"No good reason. Just...they picked a reporter at random to target today. They wanted to scare you."

"They succeeded."

He tightens his hold on me as the door opens, and I close my eyes as the police commander introduces himself to Marcus. I listen to the steady, rich buzz of his voice through his chest as he tells the supervisor what he just told me, with more details I want to not hear. In my head, I start to say *la-la-la*, and when the other cop returns with juice, I sit down at the table and down it.

Only when I set down the empty bottle do I realize that my hands are shaking.

It's another hour before we can leave. I check in with James, who says there's a new phone waiting for me at the hotel, organized by our editor. I thank him, and when we arrive at the hotel, I call our editor and thank him as well.

"Take the next day for yourself," he says.

I tell him about Marcus showing up. He knows I'm taking a few vacation days to go to the wedding, and I tell him I might go sooner than later.

"You've worked hard these last few months. Take the time you need. And Poppy?"

"Yeah."

"I'm sorry. We'll work on better barricades for future events."

"Yeah." I take a deep breath. "I'll have a personal reflection piece on today in a few days. I know you don't need one, but I'll want to write it anyway."

"Sounds good."

I hang up, then pace across the room. Marcus watches me silently.

"I used the interceptor device," I tell him. "So whoever got my phone...it won't do anything. They won't get anything."

"Good."

I pace again before finally stopping in front of him where he was sitting on the bed. "You came out to the east coast early for this, didn't you?"

He looks me right in the eye. "Sure. A little. But I also need to do some real estate hunting while I'm in New York."

"For you?"

"Not exactly."

I laugh. "You know what my favorite thing is about you?

How forthcoming you are with interesting facts and explanations. It's so refreshing—"

He cuts me off with a demanding kiss, then he tugs on my ponytail. "It's for my cousin Astrid. She has an exhibit that needs a tall, vertical space. She doubts she's going to find a gallery that can accommodate her, so we're going to use this as an opportunity to try something new with our foundation."

"Oh." That sounds cool. "What kind of exhibit?"

"It's called Climb a Mountain." He eases me onto the bed, and I roll onto my side. He fits in behind me as the big spoon and keeps talking about the exhibit, but I'm drifting again.

The next thing I know, he's quietly rubbing my wrist.

"I'm fine," I say for the hundredth time today.

"I know," he whispers. "But that was scary for me, too."

CHAPTER SIXTEEN

MARCUS

I DON'T LET Poppy out of my sight for the next five days.

I'm starting to irritate her, and I'm not sorry, not even a little.

"It wasn't that big a deal," she insists, like it matters that he only grabbed her. It's what could have happened that has me losing sleep at night.

But once we're in New York for the wedding festivities, my worry lessens. It's hard not to be happy when Jake and Jana are over the moon and intent on sharing that joy with the world. Instead of separate bachelor and bachelorette parties, they have a big rehearsal dinner followed by a grown-up pajama party, complete with board games that Jana did custom illustrations for—a touch Poppy adores.

Before the rehearsal dinner there's a riddle scavenger hunt which leads guests around the Plaza Hotel, deftly facilitating a wide cross-section of family and friends and acquaintances to meet each other by happenstance.

We end up helping Jana's friend Nina decode a riddle at in the basement, and we're rewarded with shots from her purse flask.

"I like her already," Poppy says as we head back upstairs.

I squeeze her tight.

The next morning we shower and get dressed together. I leave the tie for last, and watch Poppy do her makeup instead.

She smiles at me in the mirror. "Ready to go?"

"Yeah."

"Want me to tie your tie for you?"

"Damn straight I do."

Her laughter is still ringing in my ears as we make our way to the ballroom.

"You don't look comfortable in a suit," she whispers.

"I'm not."

She turns her head toward me. "That's too bad."

"Why's that?"

Her voice drops. "Because looking at you in a suit makes me wet."

Jesus.

Well, now.

Just ahead of us there's a bathroom, and I yank the door open, sliding us in. Good, the door locks. I flip that and press her back against the wall.

"What are you doing?" she breathes against my mouth.

"Ruining your lipstick."

"Don't you dare." But she smiles.

I kiss her lightly. Okay, we'll do this the hard way. Hovering my mouth right above hers, I pull up her skirt and slide my fingers between her legs. She's warm and soft and so damn responsive. This is what I needed to ground me. Poppy's breath against my mouth, her essence on my skin. "Shhh," I warn her, and she gasps. "I can kiss you if you need that to stay quiet."

"I'm...oh...okay." She presses her lips together and closes her eyes.

So beautiful. "Come for me, baby. Ride my fingers."

She groans and rocks her hips, her clit swelling against the heel of my hand. I need to taste her. Dropping to my knees, I lick that sweet spot at the top of her cleft, forcing my tongue against her flesh as she slowly, carefully fucks herself on my hand.

Fuck, yes.

"Come on," I urge her between licks. "Come for me."

She freezes as her sex clutches around my fingers, tight spasms that I want to feel on my cock. Later. Definitely later.

When she finishes, I lick her clean, then slide her panties back into place.

She watches me with a satisfied smile on her face as I wash my hands.

Then I prowl back to her and cage her against the wall. "You can't tell me something like that and not expect me to follow up."

She gives me an amused look. "I guess not."

"Come on, let's get this over with."

"Is that any way to talk about your best friend's wedding?" She's laughing at me. I'm desperate and she's enjoying herself.

I haul her close, pressing my erection into her belly. "Feel that?"

"Oh, yeah." She bites her lower lip.

"All I care about right now."

"So we should talk about math or something?"

"Or something. Yeah."

"I love weddings," she whispers. "Dressing up, drinking champagne...it's like a throwback to days of yore that never really existed. But it's all just so pretty. And then there's dancing."

"You want to dance tonight?" I'm all over that. "I'm your man."

"Yes you are." Her lips twitch, and I'm tempted to just fuck her right now, just because. Just to put my mark on her, to leave a bit of myself inside her for the rest of the day.

Maybe I like weddings too, in my own twisted way. At least I like this one. I like the look on Poppy's face when she talks dreamily of dancing and dressing up and champagne.

"Besides, the sooner the wedding is over, the sooner we get on the road to go meet my parents."

"You think I'm nervous about that?" My voice catches on a thick burr. Okay, I'm nervous about it, but not for any reason she might think.

For the first time in my life, I want to make a good impression on a girlfriend's family.

"Maybe not nervous..." She slides me a sly glance. "But they're going to be all over you."

"I can handle that."

"It's loud. Chaotic."

"Worse than a middle-grade field trip group?"

"At least."

I grin. "I'll manage just fine."

The wedding ceremony is short, romantic, and funny. Jake pumps his fist in the air after Jana says, "I do," and she gets teary during his vows.

More of Jana's illustrations are found in the paper details. The ceremony programs, the instructions for the cocktail hour, and then the seating chart for the reception, too. The cards at our seats are a special surprise. Jana's drawn cartoon characters for each of us. Poppy's writing in a notepad, and I'm wearing my ranger uniform.

When Jake stands to give his speech, the whole room goes quiet. "Thank you all for coming," he says, and even though he made it through the ceremony without getting choked up, now his voice sounds a little thick.

I give him a thumbs up, and he grins.

"A year ago, I embarked on a new business venture. I do that a lot, so normally this story wouldn't be anything special. But as those of you who have fallen in love know, there are these moments in time. Special, unexpected, magical things that happen. And *this* particular business venture happened to lead me to Jana's doorstep. From the first second I laid eyes on her, I knew she was the one." He breathes in an exaggerated inhale. "Sadly, she thought I was some shmuck named Marcus Dane."

My mouth drops open. I didn't know this part of the story.

And from the look on Jana's face, she didn't either.

He shakes his head and laughs at himself. "See, I was working as a SwiftEx driver, and when they asked me whose name I wanted on the uniform, I thought, shit...I can't use my real name. Just in case. So I gave them the name of one of the best men I know, my friend Marcus, who left the tech world a decade ago to do a real days' work instead. So I told them to put Dane on the name badge. Man, do you know how awkward that was?"

Jana's laughing now, and she gets up and takes the microphone. "Don't worry, Marcus, we straightened out the name thing before we got too serious."

"Phew," I say, lifting my voice.

"But anyway, that was the moment when my life changed. When I least expected it. When I wasn't even myself. And I count my blessings every single day that I went to Baltimore and chose that route, because Jana is everything to me." He takes her hand. "I love you so much, and I'm damn proud to be your husband."

Everyone raises their glasses in a toast, and Poppy and I exchange a private look.

Yes, we know what that kind of a moment is like.

And I count my blessings every day, too.

EPILOGUE

POPPY

December

I SPEND the three weeks before Christmas in Dallas, interviewing survivors of a horrific mass shooting attack that targeted police in particular. It's draining, challenging work, but the long form piece we write is something to be proud of. It's a story of hope and courage and fierce resilience.

And when I finish, I can fly directly to Grand Junction.

Marcus is waiting for me just outside the arrival gate.

"Who is this handsome man wearing a suit?" I ask him after he kisses me senseless in the middle of the terminal.

"Merry Christmas," he says as I tug on the lapels of his wool overcoat. "I skipped the tie."

"Still makes me hot."

He grins wickedly. "That was the plan. How was your flight?"

"Fine."

We exchange a private smile. It was a matter of some debate, whether or not I'd fly commercial, but he can't be my full-time bodyguard, and the paper took the security threat seriously. Nobody knew where we stayed and I kept all mention of travel dates off social media.

He carefully zips up my parka, then we head outside to his truck. It's a clear, cold night, but his truck warms up quickly.

"Tell me about Dallas," he says after we stop at Starbucks.

I sip my hot coffee and try to categorize my thoughts. "It was intense. Lots of anger, lots of sadness. No clear path forward, really, although the sense of community was clear. People really are wonderful in a time of need. I told you a little bit about that when we talked."

Every night. His constant, quiet support was something I looked forward to all day.

He squeezes my hand across the center console. "What's next?"

"I don't know. I have a week off to decorate a Christmas tree and laze in front of your wood stove."

He laughs. "So we're going to cut down a tree tomorrow?"

But when we arrive at his place, there are three presents waiting just inside the door. All big boxes, each wrapped in a different colour of shiny paper.

"Open them," he says as he strips me out of my winter coat.

"Hard to do while you're kissing me."

"I make no apologies for missing you. Go on."

"Shouldn't I wait until we have a tree for the presents to go under?"

"I've got other presents for you for then."

I rip open the red one first. Inside are adult snow pants, with a tag that says, ***For picking out the perfect Christmas tree***.

I spin around and point at him. "You."

He grins. "Me."

"With your innocent 'So we're going to cut down a tree?' question."

"Yep."

"I love you." I grab the second box and it's lighter than the first. I peel away the silver paper and peek inside, finding boxes of ornaments and a strand of white lights. ***For decorating our first Christmas tree***, the tag attached to the lights reads.

The last box is even lighter than the first two. It feels like there's nothing in it, which makes me very curious. I rip into the shiny blue wrapping paper. Inside, the box is almost empty, except for a long, rolled-up piece of paper.

I pull it out and unfurl it.

It's a map of the world, and there's a tag tapped to the corner. ***For you to pick where we spend next Christmas. Tree optional.***

"Oh, Marcus..." I spin around, the map fluttering from my hands, and he picks me up. "Right here sounds perfect."

"I don't want you to feel tied to Colorado," he rumbles as he kisses my neck. "I like it here, but I can travel."

"I know." We're going back to New York next month for his

cousin's exhibit opening. We talked about getting away to the Caribbean this winter, too. "But I'm happy here, too. I always feel a sense of calm, of rightness, when I touch down." I slide my fingers into his thick hair and press our foreheads together. "I love coming home to you."

His arms tighten around me. "Thank God."

"But I like bikinis, too, so maybe a New Year's trip next year?"

He laughs as he picks me up and carries me to the bedroom. "I'm one-hundred percent pro-bikini. That's an amazing plan."

The next morning, I pull on my new snow pants, the heavy-duty winter boots I bought last month, my parka, and one of Marcus's wool hats, and we head up the trail behind his house. It's bright and sunny, but nippy and colder than I expect.

"That sun isn't doing anything to cut the cold, is it?" I ask as Marcus zips my coat up the last inch, better protecting my neck.

He rubs my hands through my mitts. "Nope. Always colder when it's sunny."

"That's weird," I mutter.

He just chuckles. "Almost there. I scouted out a couple of trees earlier this week. All blue spruce. Depends what kind of tree you want. Fat, tall, fluffy?"

I point to a little Charlie Brown-esque tree struggling on the side of the path. "That one will do."

Marcus howls in protest and scoops up some of the snow dusting the ground. He packs it together as he walks backwards up the path.

"Are we having a snowball fight now?"

He grins. "Maybe. Arm yourself."

I crouch and gather my own snow. I make two snowballs before I stand up, and when I do, he's further ahead, almost around the bend.

"Ready?" he calls out.

"For what?"

"A chase."

But this time he's the one who takes off running.

Well, that's one way to warm me up in a hurry. I take off after him. Over the rise and down the other side, gathering speed as I run down toward the stand of trees where I'm pretty sure he's hiding.

And I'm right. A snowball flies out of the shadows at me, hitting my shoulder.

I hurl one back but it hits a tree instead of a man.

Damn it.

I skid to a stop and cut right, heading into the trees. From below me, Marcus calls out. "I see you, baby."

"Then come and get me," I holler back.

"You don't want to chase me?"

"Not if you're armed with snow balls!" I creep along, hiding behind trees each time I stop, until I see him.

He's almost looking at me, but not quite.

I take a deep breath and fire my biggest snow ball at him.

He turns just in time for it to hit him squarely in the chest.

"Got you!" I yell triumphantly.

He whips his second snowball back, and I dodge before returning volley.

Now we're both unarmed, so there's only one thing to do. I

charge toward him and he catches me as I tackle him to the ground—which is surprisingly hard.

Well, duh, it's frozen.

"Crap, are you okay?" I ask as I scramble off him.

He grunts. "Yes. Fine. Get back here." He catches my hand and tugs me down on top of him. "Nothing a few kisses can't fix," he murmurs before catching my lips with his own.

"Are you going to get a little handsy?" I ask when he rolls us onto our sides and tugs at my zipper.

"I'll warm you up, don't worry."

"That was not a worried question, I promise— Ah! Yes..." I sigh and gasp as he slides his hands into my snow pants.

"Nice and toasty," he murmurs. "So hot, Poppy."

"So dirty, Marcus."

"What did you call me when we met? A pervert?" He looks at me, his eyes dancing.

"I love that about you," I say as I roll my head back against his arm, protecting me from the ground. "So much. Oh! There!"

"I'm your pervert," he whispers in my ear as I ride his fingers. "Only for you, baby. Always for you."

"Was this all a ruse to have sex outside? Is this a Colorado tradition?"

He laughs. "It is now. But I'm still going to chop down your tree."

I whimper as I grind my clit against his hand. "That sounds like a terrible euphemism."

"Fell your pine?"

"Maybe that's something I can...do to you. After."

"After?"

"God, Marcus, make me come!"

"Since you asked so nicely..." He adds another finger and shifts his hand, stretching me inside and rolling his thumb against my clit at the same time.

I close my eyes and give myself over to the sharp, climbing pleasure. Faster, harder we rock until I shatter, Marcus's hand tight between my legs until the last spasm fades.

He helps me up, and we kiss as he leans back against a tree. Then I fall to me knees and unzip him, picking my favorite Christmas wood of all.

THE END

for Marcus and Poppy...

But Ben's story is coming, and Brianne and Marcus's cousin Astrid gets a book, too! Visit my website to keep reading! And if you want to hear about the next release in this series, or any other sexy rom com news from me, join my VIP reader list at www.smarturl.it/AinsleyMail!

ABOUT THE AUTHOR

Mom by day and filthy romance writer by night, Ainsley is a three-time USA Today bestseller (Hate F*@k, Prime Minister), and super grateful for caffeine and yoga pants. Born and raised near Toronto, Ontario, Canada, she's traveled the world and come back home to write about book boyfriends with maple leaf tattoos.

www.ainsleybooth.com
www.friskybeavers.com

ACKNOWLEDGMENTS

This story was originally written for the *Rogue Desire* anthology, a resistance romance collection I was thrilled to be a part of. Emma Barry and Tamsen Parker had the original idea on Twitter, and I'm grateful that they let me horn in, take over the cover design, and write a perverted park ranger story, too. The romance community is a wonderful thing!

ALSO AVAILABLE FROM AINSLEY BOOTH

FORBIDDEN BODYGUARDS

Hate F*@k
Booty Call
Dirty Love
First Lady, His Lady
Wicked Sin

BILLIONAIRE SECRETS

Personal Delivery
Personal Escort
Personal Disaster
Personal Interest
Personal Proposal

FRISKY BEAVERS

Retrosexual
Prime Minister
Dr. Bad Boy
Full Mountie

Mr. Hat Trick

Bull of the Woods

Cover Design by Oh So Novel

Printed in Great Britain
by Amazon

32888056R00090